TIME
WITH
CHILDREN

TIME
WITH
CHILDREN

STORIES BY
ELIZABETH TALLENT

ALFRED A. KNOPF
NEW YORK 1987

Most stories in this work were originally published in *The New Yorker.*

"Two Ghosts of Us" was originally published in *Grand Street.*

"Migrants" was originally published in *The Paris Review.*

Grateful acknowledgment is made to PEN Syndicated Fiction Project for
permission to reprint "No One's a Mystery," by Elizabeth Tallent, which
was originally published in *Newsday* and *The Cincinnati Enquirer,*
January 1985. Reprinted by permission of PEN Syndicated Fiction Project.

Library of Congress Cataloging-in-Publication Data

Tallent, Elizabeth.
    Time with children.

    A collection of short stories.
    I. Title.
PS3570.A398T5   1987   813'.54   87-45100
ISBN 0-394-55783-2

Manufactured in the United States of America
First Edition

for Bar

They chopped wood, they lit the stove, they kept busy; there is always something to do in a house.

—EDNA O'BRIEN

CONTENTS

TIME WITH CHILDREN

⟩⟩ Grant of
⟨⟨ Easement

The magpies were drawn to construction. There was something piratical in their black eyes and intent, lilting flight. Perhaps they liked the glitter of tenpenny nails driven into red tarpaper, or the flaxen sawdust billowing from the blade of the table saw, or the bolts buried like coins in the pickup's muddy tire tracks. Perhaps they simply liked the mess—the stray work glove stranded in the innermost coil of a bale of chicken wire, the shavings swept into heaps, the heaps left to unravel in the wind, the oil drums brimming with junk.

The magpies lived in the cottonwoods down along the river, and the house was set into the bluff a quarter mile away. The magpies traversed the quarter mile in fits and starts, flirting from tree to tree in Sandoval's orchard, the small apples rocking where the birds lit and sometimes thudding to the ground. Sandoval's asthmatic old dog lifted his nose and gazed hopelessly at the magpies, each one a merciless tease. Sandoval himself, ignoring the birds, would sit bent over on his wooden crate polishing an apple in his lap, hundreds of other apples, ranked by desirability, radiating out from his unlaced work

3

boots, the most nearly perfect apples touching his scuffed toes, those with worms or bruises several inches away. Sandoval had no ladder and no real wish to borrow one; borrowing was the first link in a chain of favors that would bind him to neighbors he had kept his distance from all his life. His trees had been trained into crippled scrolls of twigs, borne on dwarfed trunks of pale gray or olive in which the pruning scars were old and crude. In the rafts of clipped branches throughout the orchard, there was no apple too high for Sandoval to reach. Now the fretful shapes were obscured by shifting leaves, and Sandoval sat in their shadow. Burnishing and sorting, Sandoval passed an hour. He was so old that an afternoon was nothing to him. It passed in apples.

Jenny's husband, who was doing the renovations on the house himself and had so far finished only the kitchen, went down the hill when he wanted eggs for their breakfast. The old man's chickens were glossy and industrious, filing down the ramp of the henhouse to forage, their napes pulsing as they surveyed the warm dust, the barren rosebushes planted by Sandoval's long-dead wife, the remote pyramid of the woodpile. At dusk, Old Man Sandoval fed them from his wife's apron, a horizontal sail weighted at its center; he tried to fend off the boldest hens and reach the shyer, lagging ones. Their eggs were fawn or nearly yellow or a mild graham-cracker brown, often curiously dimpled. Sometimes bits of straw were pasted to the shells, or insect wings, or an occasional trim dark feather. The first time he went down the road after eggs, Sam took two dollars, and the old man agreed with him that that was fair for a dozen. Sam carried his paper bag up the slope to Jenny, who was just awake. Bare-legged, unbrushed, in running shorts and a torn black leotard, she counted the eggs out onto the bright butcher block of the counter Sam had finished the week before. On the un-nicked wood, ten eggs rocked or spun slowly and then grew still, anchored to their reflections. Jenny laughed softly over her shoulder.

"That can't be," Sam said.

"Only ten," Jenny said; she liked it that Sam had been taken.

"Do you think he's so old he lost count? Did you know he can't even read?"

"He told you that?"

"He told me that."

"He was softening you up," Jenny said. "He can certainly count. He cheated you." She liked it, but she didn't want it to happen to Sam again. They were the only Anglos in the neighborhood; all around them were Spanish families who had held on to their scraps of elaborately subdivided land, and that, Jenny thought, took cunning. She didn't want to go up against cunning like that. It was a risk, moving into the country; it was a risk that you would be isolated by your relatively great wealth from your neighbors, watched, and, when you left your house, selectively stolen from. It was a risk that you would have to island yourself in with dead-bolt locks and alarms, and she didn't want that to happen, or even to begin to happen. She would have to keep an eye on Sam for signs of weakness, for he had a heart more generous than hers. She often thought that of the two of them Sam was the truly married one. There was Sam, a husband to the marrow of his bones, and there was Jenny; people meeting her rarely assumed that Jenny was anyone's wife. In fact, she was a little offended if they did. Marriage often seemed to require one who was solid and reliable and one who gave the impression of not quite being bound or faithful, for whom fewer things were givens and about whom a great deal less could safely be taken for granted. That one was Jenny. She wasn't faithful even now, when they were on the brink of buying the house and so much was riding, in a sense, on fidelity.

She was having an affair with a married Jewish surgeon in Santa Fe who had fallen into a state of unrelenting gentle depression because Jenny would now be twenty-seven miles away and their hours together would be harder to come by. He had assumed it was the end. She didn't know. Maybe it was. She and Sam hadn't made love in weeks. She generally took that as a sign she ought to end whatever affair or flirtation she was involved in, when it began to erode that private terrain she thought of as hers and Sam's. Sam had drawn a charmed circle around their marriage; inside it was Jenny's narrower circle.

She rolled an egg along the counter, and Sam caught it and cracked it into the skillet. "I don't mind that he did that," he said. "I think it's funny."

"There's something you don't get, Sam."

"What's that?" A second egg, broken airily, the parted halves bound for a moment by strands.

"He won't like you if you let it happen again. It's impossible to really like someone you can take advantage of," Jenny said.

A third egg skated across the black iron. "Why not?"

"It just is. Like it's impossible to be generous to a miser; some quality of miserliness rules it out. Sandoval wants to take things, not be given them. He doesn't see that the few pennies' difference could not possibly matter to you. In his eyes, pennies have to matter. So you're the loser."

"I'm feeling greedy," Sam said; he cracked a fourth egg. He collected the shells, nesting one inside another, and dropped them into the garbage can in the corner.

"Don't break the yolks, Sam."

"Maybe he needs the two dollars."

"He needs to know that you respect his eggs. He needs to know that more than he needs the two dollars. If you don't count them, it's as if they're not valuable to you. He's testing you, can't you see that?"

"I think that's what you see." A hissing from the skillet as Sam prodded with the spatula.

"Promise you won't go down there again unless you're going to count the eggs."

"Look, Jen, if he doesn't give me a dozen, I'll break his arthritic old arm for him. Good enough?"

Jenny stood softly shaking her head.

It was fall, and there was still a great deal of unfinished business to do with the buying of the house. Jenny and Sam had a lease-purchase agreement, drawn up by their lawyer, allowing them to make any changes they wanted in the house, but in Jenny's eyes it was still only a glorified lease, and they'd sunk a lot of money into the renovations. The remaining problems were those invented, Jenny said to herself—*invented*—by the title company.

The last obstacle to closing had to do with obtaining a grant of easement. Easement in this case meant access to the land. The two women who were selling the house to Jenny and Sam had owned it for twenty years. They were aging cousins who had chosen to live together, and the first time Jenny saw the inside of the house, there had been in their slightly vexed hospitality a quality she named later in the car for Sam: genteel poverty. Years ago, the two cousins had quieted the title, and essentially Jenny felt safe. She felt safe because the cousins badly wanted to sell the property, and they badly wanted to sell it to Jenny and Sam, not least because they wished whoever lived in the house after them to fill it with the sound of pattering little feet. Jenny hadn't disillusioned them. She didn't want children yet, but she didn't *not* want them. The other reason she felt safe was that it was possible to go to court and prove that there already existed, as access to the land, something known as prescriptive easement: a road to the house had been used by the people who lived there for years, so the consent of the neighbors to the use of the road was implied. But this wasn't the same, to the title company, as a true grant of easement, which must be signed by any neighbor along the road.

The neighbor at the bottom of the hill, owning land on both sides of the dirt road, orchards of long grass and crippled trees now beginning to lose their leaves, was Sandoval.

Jenny sat in the office of the title company with her fists in her lap. There was industrial carpeting on the floor and O'Keeffe's *Two Jimson Weeds* on the wall. There were hand-glazed coffee cups for three. On the desk of the woman facing her was the survey of the land, the house, the road, and Sandoval's flanking orchards.

"Will Mr. Sandoval be agreeable?" Ms. Levitt, the title-company woman, asked. "He's the only possible problem. The road crosses the *acequia*"—she tapped the minute bridge with the eraser of a pencil—"but the irrigation-ditch committee should be fine. You must get signatures from the president, the vice-president, and the secretary, all three. But they're used to that sort of thing. Now, what do you think of our Mr. Sandoval?"

"He's not ours," Jenny said.

"I beg your pardon?"

"There's no problem that I can see," Sam said, "except the small problem that Mr. Sandoval can't read."

"Mr. Sandoval can't read," Ms. Levitt said. "Mr. Sandoval cannot read, is that correct?"

"No, that is not correct," Jenny said. Sam looked at her. "Mr. Sandoval can read. It's only that he needs glasses."

"Glasses. Well, needing glasses doesn't give you any problems legally. As long as he has his glasses on when he reads the document." Ms. Levitt pretended to settle a pair of spectacles on her sharp nose. Jenny didn't like this; it was a violation of Ms. Levitt's essential seriousness.

"And if he can't read, that gives us problems legally," Sam said.

"I should say so," Ms. Levitt said. "Though I am not at all sure what the extent of your problems would be there."

"They could be bad, though."

"I wouldn't like to speculate on that," she said. "I don't get paid to speculate here. I'm not a lawyer. I think you must simply pursue your grant-of-easement agreement with Mr. Sandoval. You must simply obtain his signature as soon as possible, you see, and it must be witnessed by a notary public, of course. I think we could then set a date for closing. Sellers would be agreeable to that, I think. Sellers seem most flexible."

"We're all flexible," Sam said. "As it happens."

Ms. Levitt cleared her throat. "That should be it," she said. "That is your last remaining problem. Not such a very big problem, is it?" And she looked straight at Jenny.

In the parking lot, Jenny snarled at her Volkswagen, and after two tries got it started. Sam leaned into the window. They had come in separate cars so that she could go shopping afterward. Sam looked down at Jenny's stockinged knees. "I'm just anxious, Sam," she said. "I'm just, you know, wound up. I hated her, I hate having problems. I can't stand living in a construction zone. I can't stand for *one more thing* to go wrong with this house. Your house."

"It's not my house, Jen. We're going to live there for years. You'll see."

"You're the one that's so in love with it. You're the one that's doing everything."

"Jen." He stroked the hair away from her forehead.

Usually she liked it when he did that; usually it could make her give in. Now she said sullenly, "What?"

"You'll love it, too. I want you to come home."

"I'm going shopping. I'm going to stay in town for a little while, O.K.? I just need—" She spread her hands. Sam watched the space widening between them.

Jenny went and cried on her lover's shoulder. He caught her chin (a thing she didn't like) to make her look at him and said, "Jenny, Jenny, Jenny, I want you to meet my children. It can all happen. Things can change."

She thought how much she would hate having lunch with his three daughters, their father's brown eyes gone alert, following her every move. They'd know. Of course they'd know.

"It's just the way things with the house keep dragging on," she said. "Nothing else. I have to be home before dark."

He saw that she wanted to let him down gently. He made love to her on the couch in the corner of his office, where, she thought, patients often got the bad news. Why shouldn't he? She stared at the acoustic tile of his ceiling and his Calder mobile. *I can't see you anymore* was on the tip of her tongue. Making love to her, he was already nostalgic for making love to her, yet he was, she thought, a little perfunctory about her orgasm, like a doctor who instructs you to cough.

⟨ Jenny was on her second cup of coffee before Sam was out of bed the next morning. To celebrate, she took his coffee to him. Asleep, he was entirely familiar. He slept in an old shirt, its tail wrinkled up to show his back, with the tan ending high, like the waist of his Levi's. Jenny, barefoot on the cold floor, felt guilt, subtly compounding. Something in the way that he was half dark and half pale made him seem vulnerable. The windows of the room were deep and framed in rough-cut fir, set into the east wall. Jenny watched a magpie land on a crooked fence post just on the other side of the window. It looked at her and made begging Siamese-cat cries. "You want in," Jenny told it.

In the kitchen again, she sat on the architect's stool pulled up to the counter, her nightgown sleeves pushed up, the white china cup and saucer between her elbows, her chin in her hands. She could see the overgrazed mesas, dun and ocher and almost yellow, eroded in folds and tucks like the cortex of a brain, leading down to the river, where there was a ragged mist. The sun had thinned the mist from the banks until the cottonwoods were visible and had burned it away completely from the hummocky fields, leaving them glistening wet.

Sam stood behind her. He put his hands on either side of her neck and began to rub her shoulders. "I'm taking the paper down to Sandoval," he said.

She felt lazy; she leaned back into his hands. She could feel the friction of her hair against his bare chest. "It's awfully early," she said.

"He gets up at an unbelievable hour," Sam said. "Before light."

"He's not human."

"You don't know. Old people wake up early. And he probably always has anyway—this is the country. Close your eyes."

She did. She was curious about the inside of Sandoval's house. It was of the old L-shaped architecture that meant the inner angle of the house was almost always in shade—his wife had grown roses there—and the roof was of corrugated tin, which brimmed with light like an empty mirror. Sandoval kept his yard swept and his shades drawn.

Sam worked on the muscles of her shoulders. "I'm going to cheat on the notary public," he said. "I'm going to take it in to Corey Archer over at the bank and have him sign it. He owes me a favor, and a third person in the room would only throw Sandoval off."

"Is his house cold in winter?" she said.

"Come and see. I'm sure your presence will sway him."

"He's a selfish old man, Sam. He's not going to think I'm anyone. He doesn't think you're anyone—no one is anything to him. He cares about eggs." She giggled. "He cares about apples."

"He cares about his dog."

"Then that's the only living thing."

"You've got such a cold heart, Jenny."

"No, I don't." But she felt suddenly wounded, and sat upright. "Take that back."

"I take it back, O.K.?"

It wasn't, quite.

In boots and straight-legged jeans and an old navy sweater of Sam's unraveling at the cuffs, Jenny went down the hill. Sam held her hand. She read his watch: "It's only *seven*."

It was dark in the kitchen of Sandoval's house. Jenny could see a handsome antique cookstove over the old man's shoulder when he came to the door. The stove had recently been lit, its narrow door left open on its hinges; sparks rained out, disappearing in midair. It looked as if a tiny meteor were burning in a deep cave. Sandoval went over to the stove, crumpled a page of newspaper and fed it in, following this with several twigs and a wide red sliver of cedar. In his gestures he was slow and entirely methodical, as if he were alone. Jenny breathed deeply: coffee and kindling, iron heating up and a faint scent of struck matches. The adobe walls had once, long ago, been touched with pink whitewash, a ghost of rouge that went oddly with the somber russet of the wood, in which the fluting of pressed fingers was still dimly visible. A stained enamel sink with a rolled lip like that of an ancient bathtub; a counter of linoleum tiles, corners curled up to show the black and slightly greasy sealing compound; a coffee cup with a chipped handle, a spoon resting inside the cup, and a dishrag coiled by it as if the counter had just been washed. The old man's dog, its nose beneath its tail, slept in the corner by the stove, where charred spots dappled the pine floor. There was the smell of poverty, but also of objects thoughtfully cared for—a hoarded and extremely silent life. She could not condescend to it. Yet that was one of her impulses: recognizing that this was so made her uneasy. The old man scraped a chair across the floor. She didn't understand until Sam said softly, "Sit down." She did.

Sam smoothed the paper on the oilcloth. Among the cracks and worn patches there were roses on a trellis. "Mr. Sandoval," Sam said, "this is a paper I'd like for you to sign. I'll read it to you:

> I, Esteban Sandoval, a single man, hereby grant unto Samuel J. Small and Jennifer A. Small, their heirs, successors, and assigns, a non-exclusive perpetual easement for ingress, egress, and utilities over, across, and under the following described parcel of land situated within the County of Santa Fe, State of New Mexico."

Then followed the surveyor's boundary measurements, which Sam read twice. "That means our land," he said. "As far as that fallen barbed wire in the north corner, and the juniper stump on the slope, and then down to the arroyo, and touching Delgado's on the other side. But this is the numbers for it."

Sandoval listened all the way through, and then he nodded. Jenny held her breath. "*Bueno*," he said. "It's O.K. by me. Only I don't have a pencil here." He seemed shamed when he said this.

"I have one," Sam said.

The old man caressed the fountain pen and knotted his horny hand around it. Jenny could see that he had arthritis: his thumb would not close against his fingers, but jutted out stubbornly, and the fan of skin between thumb and forefinger was pulled taut. He slid the paper toward him until its bottom edge rested against his bib overalls, and studied it for a moment. He wrote cautiously, in long, linked, scrolling letters, painfully, hiding the pain, taking his time. When he was finished, he drew a sort of flourishing line that linked the capitals of his first and last name. The nail of his jutting thumb was yellow and opaque as quartz. He pushed the paper toward Sam. "Look all right to you?"

The signature was very gloomy and archaic. It wobbled above and below the line that the title company's clerk had typed for it, and the final "l" ended in a tendril, cramped to fit, which nonetheless slanted off the page. "Thank you," Sam said.

"Yes, thank you," Jenny said. She had a curious sensation of pity, as if they were his children and he had grown old before their eyes, as if they had drained him of something. His eyelashes were of a paleness that made the lids seem naked, but his glance at her was utterly direct, and in the faded tobacco-brown of each iris the blue-black pupil was clear.

"We won't keep you from your morning any longer," Sam said.

"You're not keeping me from much," he said. "And if there was anything, you wouldn't be keeping me from it."

He pushed himself up and escorted them into the front yard, chickens scattering before them. He was somewhat shorter than Jenny, and this made her feel lumbering and discourteous. He left them for a moment. They waited, Sam beating the signed paper lightly against his leg, until Sandoval returned with something in his hand, cradling it against the front of his overalls as if to keep them from seeing what it was. He glanced severely at Jenny. She reached out, and he tipped the two eggs delicately into her hand.

"Thank God someone taught him to sign his name," Sam said when they were on the road. Then he sang, a little mockingly, "Our house is a very, very, *very* fine house."

"I'm so pleased," Jenny said.

"Are you?" Sam said. "Did you see him keep my pen? My good gold fountain pen?"

"He's a fox," Jenny said. "The eggs are lovely. I want to keep them. I want them never to break."

She walked up the hill, holding the two eggs the way the old man had held them, to her breast—to warm them or be warmed, she couldn't have said.

The
Fence
Party

With the sound of the river forcing him to lift his voice and pitch it for her ears, Hart is holding forth to a woman with doctored auburn hair on the eccentricities of his father-in-law, a Nicaraguan refugee. She inclines her head, an angle that mimics, and in a shady way pretends to predict, intimacy. She has such a small, guarded face, crowned with the absurd hair, that he wants her to come closer. As a subject, fathers-in-law are a little poignant: Hart knows that this woman has had at least two. Acknowledging his own father-in-law proves that Hart is a family man. He likes to establish that at once and let his amused account, falling into the gentlest irritation, suggest that he might be a slightly disappointed family man. That is the second thing Hart likes to make known. He likes to present the fact and the subtle hint of its contradiction together, a knot.

All afternoon, from a distance, Hart followed the auburn head among his guests, who had been invited to mend the old fence on the steep slope above the house. He watched her swinging a hammer, riding forward on its strokes with a carpenter's grace, her tanned, barefoot daughter handing her tenpenny nails, and fell in love. The party is a reward for the fence's menders, and a housewarming as well, because Hart and his second wife, Caro, bought the house last winter, less than a month after they were married. He is lucky in the weather, as he knew he would be. Only last week, the evening would have been too cold for people to stand around drinking on the lawn. But not tonight, not when everyone feels flushed and high with work. Tonight could almost be summer.

Hart puts his hand on the woman's arm, then knows that was a mistake, and pretends, working thumb and forefinger, to rub out a mosquito. He does voices well and has caught the Nicaraguan lilt exactly, more exactly than the auburn head can take in. Hart's brother-in-law works in a windowless Washington cubicle, and once Hart tricked him, long distance, into believing that he was a desperate, but definitely Nicaraguan, refugee. It was too bad he did that, because Caro found out. She interpreted it to mean that he didn't believe in the serious nature of her brother's work; that he took the entire Dominguez family far too lightly; that she should pack and go before she was ever so shamed in her family's eyes again. If she happened to overhear him now, she would guess exactly what he was up to. Hart glances over his shoulder. Caro is standing on the reedy bank, out of earshot, stripping a willow twig and letting the leaves wing down into the current, fast with snowmelt. Beside her, an elderly guest in baggy trousers scans the river for teal with Caro's binoculars; Caro must have told him what to search for. It's a good thing that in bird-watching Caro has found something she likes. Hart hadn't known how she would handle the solitude of the house in the gorge. He teaches mathematics three days a week, fifty miles each way, and those nights it's easiest for him to sleep on the couch in his office. But in the intense, close Dominguez clan of brothers, sisters, godparents, and cousins, no one is ever by himself, and at first Caro was frightened of the house's remoteness—of the way that up and down the canyon at night there were no lights that were not stars. Lately, though, Hart has almost ceased to worry about her. Last month when the river began to rise, she spent the days dragging and stacking sandbags into a wall that now protects the house, tapering away along the lawn's undercut, somewhat treacherous bank. Because they were meant to hold wheat for famine relief, the hundreds of dun sandbags had DONATED BY THE PEOPLE OF THE U.S.A. printed on them, and, for longshoremen, USE NO HOOKS. Caro had even been in the paper—a grainy, dramatic photograph of a young woman, her arms streaked with mud, fortifying her house against the rising Rio Grande.

No one knows how badly Hart wanted this house on the river. Not Caro, and not Kevin, Hart's fifteen-year-old son, who reads his father's emotions with uncanny and troubling accuracy. But Caro and Kevin would never have suspected Hart of such single-mindedness, though in fact he was intent on having the house as soon as he saw it, from the intaglio Moorish cross on the granite threshold, through each of the quiet, cobwebbed rooms, to the chicken coop on the slope. He felt a sharp nostalgia when the door rocked open at the real estate agent's prodding to reveal the downy floor of the abandoned coop, with rays of light smoking in between the warped pine planks. Silent with covetousness, back in the shadowy living room, Hart let the agent run through her pitch, but nothing she said mattered to him. He was already sold.

To his surprise, Caro was game. She adapted. Slugging leaden sandbags into place, she had had lots of time to feel furious regret at being tied to an old house in danger of washing away, but she'd been uncomplaining, even stoic. She deserves her picture in the paper; yes, she does.

While he deserves this guest, and with a flirting dance step moves a little nearer. Her daughter looks something like her, only new-minted. The daughter's hair must be the original, brushed away from the brown forehead and falling down her back in a long mare's-tail mass, the kind of hair that would snap when brushed and has a glossy warmth that the mother, twice divorced, still tries for. This is the girl that his son has been courting all afternoon with an awkwardness that makes Hart catch his breath, he recalls so much when he sees it. Kevin pursued the girl across the lawn, along the cobbled-together fence, which they pretended to inspect, and up the river into the cottonwoods. Watching them go, Hart felt all of his amused detachment from Kevin vanish. He has Kevin all summer, but throughout the school year Kevin lives with his mother, and Hart wishes he could keep him longer, for some of the changes in Kevin are disturbing—a kind of vague depression, yet a cockiness, a screwed-up *some*thing. Kevin carries a Skoal can in a back pocket of his Levi's, where it has worn a little halo of lightness in the denim; Hart wonders if there is really chewing tobacco in the can. When he talks to Kevin lately, he feels Kevin's attention shy away, glance back, and swing toward opposition. Recently, Kevin informed Hart that he wanted to change his name to Cisco. Caro laughed, and adopted it at once. That is pure Caro, to turn against Hart in a way that seems to ally her with Kevin but actually doesn't have Kevin's best interests at heart at all. Hart has been critical of her: she doesn't lift a finger to interrupt the wary arguments.

"We're not used to each other," Caro said. "I can't be strict with him, Hart. It makes me feel like an idiot. Discipline, that's your business, if you want to act that way with him. From me he can count on empathy. That's how it goes in my family—the men for strictness, the women for empathy. Who needs it more than a fifteen-year-old kid with this strange imported stepmother?"

"It's not empathy if you just give without thinking what's good," Hart said.

"I don't understand why even little things about Kevin drive you so crazy. He doesn't do anything wrong, Hart. He even remembers your birthday." That was so: there, on the living-room wall, was the painting Kevin did when his father turned forty-three, of a tall, Kevin-like punk rocker in a funereal black suit, with skinny legs, bronze hair, and pointy sunglasses. "See, Kev has a sense of humor about himself. About you, too."

"If you're my wife, you have to begin to act like his mother," Hart snapped. For which he got what he had expected, a longish Caro stare.

Now Caro works her way through the party: an instinctive hostess, she clearly adores each guest. After all, these friends had turned up when needed, to help mend the fence; they have the rare sensation of feeling that they are people who can be counted on. Caro tends that mood, carrying a bottle of Spanish champagne to some stragglers, flushing a little laughter from them. Hart feels an abrupt, cherishing regard for his wife. What more can he ask for?

The answer to that is standing beside him, and he keeps talking.

"See, Spanish is so strange that a vital insult can sometimes be an endearment. Like *'cabrón'*—a very bad word that means 'goat.' That can be mortal. But my father-in-law, he calls me *cabrito*."

"Little goat," the auburn-haired guest says.

"Except when he calls me *chico. Chico* this, *chico* that, because *'chico'* is basically an all-purpose word, a pleasant way of ending sentences."

"My daughter had a boyfriend who called her *chica*. I was kind of worried about that. That went on for a while."

"Worried because he was Spanish?"

"And for other reasons." She touches a diamond earring. "They broke up and she just, she just didn't handle it too well. But I think he was mean to her."

Somehow, he is losing her attention. "How was he mean?"
"In little ways. You know." She turns. "Hart, *look*. In the
water." But he's gazing at her, and she does a curious thing:
she takes his chin and faces his eyes at the river. On the dark
surface, not thirty feet out, there is a floating scrap he slowly
recognizes as a forehead. The forehead of a stricken face, a
woman's, and then a second face, a man's, turning in slow
motion to stare at the party on the lawn. An overturned canoe
bucks below their arms, and seems to grind against them. Hart
is sure he sees the woman flinch. Her thin arms rest on the
canoe's underside, which threatens to throw her off. Hart thinks,
she wishes she could just lay her head down and go to sleep,
turning her cheek to the slick wood and holding on until she
lets go. He thinks, she could die. She is just so tired she could
die. Behind him, a guest calls out, "Can't you swim?"

The sound carries across the water.

The man's face, with its drenched hair, lifts, and he calls
back, "No."

Hart doesn't feel as frightened for him as for the woman.
He hands his wineglass to the auburn-haired guest, who says,
"Go on. *Go!*"

On the torn bank, with the familiar muck squishing under
his sneakers and a tier of submerged sandbags before him, Hart
tries to judge the best way of diving in among the sharp under-
water boulders, fallen long ago from the gorge's walls. He
knows what the boulders are like near the bank, because except
when the river is this high they're exposed. There is a conversation going on between the canoe, still upriver, and the lawn,
but Hart can't make it out. The man in the water has roused
himself, and is doing all the talking for the couple. Hart can see
the woman's glistening head, her cheek lying against the russet
wood now. The man begins to resist, according to the instruc-
tions of a guest on the lawn, who is calling, "Bring it around!
Bring it around!" trying to brake the canoe's speed by kicking

against it. The canoe wobbles, and the woman looks up, scared to death.

Then, with a father's alertness to the shape of his son, Hart sees a half-naked Kevin launch himself from a steep boulder so surely that his back, flat over the water, branches with muscle, and his extended arms sweep forward, hiding his face. The river takes him with slapped-up light. An amazing shock—not a stillness but a live shock—startles Hart's chest. Kevin went in thirty feet upstream from the canted canoe. Hart forgets the rocks and dives. His body knows that it wasn't a good dive, and his outstretched hands pat down the plush side of an old boulder that looms up too near his forehead. There is a dappled, wavering radiance that is the river's surface; below that, everything is a thousand shades of brown. Hart strokes strongly through the moving cold. A small voice in the back of his skull is calling, *Kevin Kevin Kevin.* Another, rational voice is reasoning that Kevin is safe. Desperate to breathe, Hart feels the mistakes his son could make. Hart remembers, from long ago, his son's impossibly clumsy adoration of the girl. He's a child, and the water is so strong. Hart strains to believe what he knows—that Kevin isn't safe, that he is somewhere in the river. Hart pushes himself against the current, and when he comes up, a window shatters. He shakes his head harshly, flinging water from his eyes, sucking air. A kind of gold-shot dusk from the river lies over everything. His gut is all springy and young with panic, and he feels very strange. He turns around in a circle. There is no canoe.

There is no Kevin. A voice calls, *Kev Kev Kev.* The wall of the gorge tilts very slowly—slowly but definitely, it rocks forward and back. Hart knows that the gorge's wall is eternal, but he saw it tilt. That dazzle in the corner of his vision is the river wrinkling around reeds. The bitterness in his mouth is the licked-clamshell taste of river water. On a gust of adrenaline, he kicks himself through another complete, more careful circle, because logic dictates that the canoe is either before him or behind him, and that he has missed it. There are some guests on the bank, still holding their glasses. The violence of his emotions buoys him up, but he is sliding rapidly downstream, away from the party.

With a rush of relief, he finds the canoe—and Kevin towing it in to the bank, almost home. The man and the woman are still clinging to the canoe, not helping. Hart hopes they're at least not hurting. Kevin's face has the awed expression of profound exertion. Kevin catches a firm hold near the bank, hooking an elbow around a willow trunk and snugging himself in, out of the full force of the current, drawing the canoe after him only when he's safe, and there. *Good boy*, Hart thinks. The man, then the woman begin to push themselves up thinly, having got their footing. Neither of them helps Kevin with the canoe, but someone on the bank is thinking and comes down to steady it while Kevin shoves. Then several other guests stride down, and there is a kind of choreographed silent-movie struggle to draw the canoeists and canoe from the water. Kevin lurches shyly out, six feet of bare-backed, bright-white boy, and Hart could sing.

He treads through another cold circle, for joy. The shadows of the cottonwoods, thrown across the river's bronze-brown, are almost touching him now. His wet head draws a haze of gnats, so close that when he blinks several are caught in his eyelashes. He dives and strokes in the direction of the lawn. When he surfaces again, he knows Kevin is looking for him among the partygoers and, not finding him there, is frightened that his father hadn't—somehow hadn't—seen the rescue. When Kevin faces the water, Hart is already wading up through the muck below the bank he dived from. His left foot is bare; between his toes, the mud is velvet. Hart hugs himself and slaps his rib cage on either side.

He climbs the stepped sandbags, then labors up the bank, patting the canoe as he passes it. He knows that the canoeists will be shepherded through the party to Caro, and that she will be very good at comforting them, and that there will be a story in it to be relayed from Dominguez to Dominguez across North America. Exultant, Hart moves through what's left of the party. The nearly drowned look awkward, like absurdly late guests. The man rather delicately cracks a can of Dos Equis, and is forced to laugh at himself for the sheer ordinariness of the thing he has just done. He has opened a beer. He could have drowned.

Caro brings a brandy for the woman, who is already feathering her spiky hair away from her face, life and vanity returning, though there are exhausted smudges under her eyes. Hart wants her to look at him, and she does. He guesses she feels a lot of things: embarrassment, pleasure in recognizing him, gratitude, anxious relief, and shock—still, prominently, shock, with shock's cold simplicity. He remembers her cheek laid against the rocking wood. He feels too close to her to try to talk to her. Caro seems to be teaching her how to drink, anyway. The woman takes the brandy in slow, breathy sips.

Hart sees the auburn-haired guest from the corner of his eye, and she gives him a big melancholy grin and swoons backward into the arms of a tennis pro, who catches her neatly. The near-drowning has brought out a rising hilarity in the guests. They are cautious about intruding on the canoeists, yet no one looks away from them, either. The canoeists are so wet they might as well be naked, but it's a charmed, neutral nakedness: no one could make them feel it. No one wishes to be very far from them. They're a little magic.

Before the banalities begin, the harmless things everyone is going to feel compelled to say, Caro catches up with Hart and says softly, "Just because *I* had *my* picture in the paper," and pounds her fist gently against his slick chest. She picks the sodden T-shirt away from his skin, but it sticks again, and she kisses his chest through it, whispering, "O.K., you're a hero now. A hero. Was it worth it?"

He's not a hero. He's abashed, and somehow banished from grace, like all of the others who didn't go in. Twenty feet away, in a clearing among the guests, Kevin is lying on his back in the grass, the wet jeans gleaming on his legs. The girl kneeling beside him is drying his face with her hair.

Hart can taste it, himself saying to his son, "Jesus, Kev, I thought I'd lost you."

Caro hits him. "Oh, no, you don't," she says. "You just leave them alone."

Time
with
Children

The cat had been rubbed the wrong way by too many strangers at too many teatimes for any human being to delight it ever again, so it lived for the small flaunting fauna, from closet moths to dingy city starlings, that turned up in the corners or on the cold outer windowsills of the flat. The cat belonged to an elderly English couple who had gone to South Africa to visit cousins, leaving the cat and seven cheerless Edwardian rooms to the Americans, knowing that was not the same as leaving them in good hands. There was no question that the American husband and wife had been made subtly aware of this, and of their great luck in having obtained the flat when they had a four-year-old boy in tow. From South Africa there were letters, some in the Englishman's schoolboy script and some in his wife's haggard scrawl, full of bits of advice, wan jokes meant to ingratiate, and admonitions about the kind of care deserved by really fine Oriental carpets. All of which the American wife blithely neglected to answer, as the English husband had dourly warned his wife she would.

After two months the cat could tell from the young woman's

voice in the kitchen when it was about to be fed. Then, after
the irregular metallic scrolling of the can opener, the cat settled
before its dish to gaze into the sheen of empty china; only a
finger to its throat could have discovered its purr. The salmon
plopped down in front of the cat's nose, and the woman began
to mash it with the tines of a fork, saying to herself, "Yuck,
yuck, *oh*, yuck." Finished, she washed her hands, sniffed them,
and washed again while calling something into the sitting room.
Though the cat was eating, its ears kinked into sharp angles:
the woman's voice, the child's, the woman's, the child's—rising
into a howled "No-o-o-o," so that the cat crouched protectively
over its bowl.

The woman's: "You know we go to parties sometimes,
Nicholas."

"*Why* do you?"

"You know we can't stay home all the time."

"*Why* can't you?"

The woman imagined answering, "We just can't," but because "We just can't" or something very like it had been used
on her as a child, she stopped; she had set herself to be original
with her son. She faced her reflection in the darkened window
of the kitchen that was so cold she had kept her coat on, feeding
the cat. Her very fine, dark hair had been cut asymmetrically,
and lay along her jaw, on one side, inches shorter than on the
other. Suddenly this looked pathetic to her. She tipped her head
to the left to make the hair fall away, testing angles until the
sides seemed even, listening vaguely while her husband took
over trying to reason with the child. There was a guest in the
sitting room as well, and they (the American family) seemed
intent on making a complicated three-way scene in front of
him. This guest was English, and Kyra doubted there was anything he would dislike more than being involuntary witness to
a family quarrel. Shaking his hand, she had felt his alert English
reserve, and been charmed by it, yet imagining his emotions

now, she was abruptly, absurdly brimming with resentment against him: Who was he, this gingerly bachelor, to judge them for their little squall? He lived alone, having had relationship after relationship, letting them all fall apart; nothing could be further from her life, or her husband's. She and Charlie had to be very, very careful with what had required, over time, such a wealth of true forgiveness, because of Charlie's various lovers.

Charlie was an editor, on loan from New York to a publisher in Bedford Square. For a year he was supposed to observe English publishing and learn. Kyra liked the idea, because that was the element of Charlie's character most in need of development: the perceptive, empathic self that could pick up on nuances. But part of why they had come to London, the saddest part, was to leave behind someone Charlie was beginning to be interested in.

Kyra went into the sitting room, sat in an armchair, slouched, and ran her fingers furiously through her hair. It was self-parody—the wife as sulking child—which an American would have got, but the English guest only appeared vague. No, he looked polite, she decided. That was that glazed expression —English politeness. Her hair had been cut that morning by a boy with cobalt-blue spikes and a bad squint, and she knew now she should never have let him come near her. She hated herself, and as always when she hated herself, hatred lapped in Charlie's direction. Look at Charlie's English friend, his stare directed with distressed courtesy at his own shoes; he had hardly been here twenty minutes, and already she had made him wish he could leave. He probably hadn't even noticed her haircut—his own was queer enough, a close-cropped, fair burr that exposed too much pale forehead. His nose was a long English nose that began in a delicate knuckle of bone and ended in a sharp, inquisitive tip, his mouth was small and closed in by lines that suggested his smile would be clever and quick, though he'd yet to smile. He'd yet even to meet her eye.

She looked from him to Charlie, whose glossy dark head was bent over his son's. God, she thought, how *pretty* Americans are, how straight their noses and even their teeth. The guest was a playwright, and this awkward visit a kind of domestic coup for Charlie, who wanted English friends. When he first met Brian, Charlie came home with a description meant to enchant Kyra into having him over for dinner: Brian kept his "a"s haughtily flat, answered the phone with four singsong digits, said "figger" for "figure," "on the trot" for "in a row," and "gulls" for "girls." Girls: Brian went out with lots, and couldn't seem to settle down with any of them—which made him exactly the kind of male friend, Kyra reflected, that Charlie loved finding. These stories of Brian's one-night stands continued until a girl turned up—Pippa, an actress—who couldn't be taken lightly, and Charlie began coming home with Pippa stories, detailing the curiously cool and equivocal (because English? because Brian told it that way?) affair. Charlie was for Pippa, Kyra was against her. Charlie reported that she was on the dole, her voice cracked like an adolescent boy's and hindered her in getting parts, her eyes were wonderful, and she paid none of the bills when she and Brian went out. Kyra wondered at her greeny, errant prickle of jealousy when she heard that Pippa's voice cracked, when for the first time Pippa was real to her. She wondered at it, and she kept it to herself, and she made up ingenious excuses when Charlie wanted to have the couple over. The truth was simply too small-minded for her to accept, and she couldn't have voiced it: Kyra didn't want Pippa in her house. Then late this afternoon Charlie had hurried in the door with what he said was wretched news. Pippa was gone. Worse still, Pippa had told Brian that he had not really loved her at all; the accusation had gone to Brian's heart.

Kyra had put her forehead against Charlie's shirt. The smell of his shirt was the smell of husbandly steadiness; suddenly she thought of a thousand ways she could be better to him. "She wanted to hurt him," Charlie said. "She said he was emotionally frigid."

"Poor Brian." She turned her face up. "So you?"

"Told him what I think, which is that Pippa has serious problems."

"I thought you *loved* her."

"You should have seen him, Ky. I've hardly ever seen anyone so lost. I told him it was probably Pippa's problems that had kept him from feeling entirely, uh, engaged."

"I think that's right," Kyra said with satisfaction. It turned out that she *was* going to see him: Charlie had told Brian to come over for drinks that evening, and there was a big publisher's party they would all go to later.

She didn't think Brian looked particularly lost, but she didn't know how to ease him from his silence either, so she and Charlie went on waiting for the sitter, with that shared anxiety oppressively clear to husband and wife but presumed by them to be invisible to anyone else, Kyra in the black Issey Miyake coat that gave her shoulders an improbable squared-off hardness, Charlie impatiently swinging a leg. He had hated waiting for sitters since Nicholas's first, who had left *The Story of O* tucked under the cushion of Charlie's favorite armchair. Kyra resented this impatience, because she had chosen the sitter and she knew that Charlie would get it worked around until, in his mind, the wait was her fault. But as they sometimes did, they were pretending to be several notches happier than they were, this time for Brian's benefit. Brian was leaning forward, his elbows on his knees, watching Nicholas draw. Nicholas, flat on his stomach, his face close to his coloring book, was hiding his pleasure at being observed. The phone gave its double English ring, and as

Kyra answered, she followed the changes in Charlie's expression
—interested, angry, and then freezing into disappointment as
she hung up.

"That was guess who." She shook her head. "Not a very
brilliant excuse, not even very apologetic. In fact, I think she
was rude to me."

"Will you hold this?" Nicholas said. "I can't." He handed
Brian a sparkly gold crayon.

"If she's that reliable, it's a good thing we're not leaving
Nicholas with her. So that's it, huh? That's the ballgame. An
Americanism," Charlie added for Brian.

"I know." Brian handed the gold crayon to Nicholas, who
had made a waiting platform of his palm. "Look, it seems stupid
your getting dressed up for nothing. I'll stay here. You two
go on."

"We can't ask you to do that," Charlie said—which, to
Kyra, meant that he liked the idea.

"You didn't ask. I've volunteered. After all, it was to be
Kyra's first English party, wasn't it?"

She said quickly. "That's all right."

"I've been to masses of these things. And tonight I'm not
sure you could say I'm up for it."

The party was something Charlie badly wanted to make
an appearance at; he cleared his throat.

"I don't think," Kyra said, "that we should take advantage
of Brian that way, Charlie. N-I-C-H-O-L-A-S has been difficult."
Still, Brian's offer seemed to be genuine; there was nothing
forced in his amused glance at her, and nothing bored. He hadn't
shaved, but she knew that the nonshaving had nothing to do
with grief over Pippa but was dictated by the same fashion that
had decreed the cruel, prison-camp haircut. Intelligent English
men seemed determined to look ruined.

"You would not be taking advantage," he said.

His stubble didn't match his hair, being much darker, lying

smooth along his jaw but scratchily uneven on his upper lip. She wondered what class he was. All of that was obscure to her. "Yes, we would," she said, and slanted her eyes at her son.

"Look, I don't get to be around children much, and I do get to go to publishers' parties. I can tell you now each failed witticism, every cautious advance, every spurning."

Not handsome, not at all, and she liked handsome men, yet when she tried to imagine him handsomer, she found that the angular oddness of his clever face insisted on itself. "I never see English men flirt," she said, and was interested to find her look steadily held and returned.

"He means, advances by editors to writers, Kyra."

It was she who looked away. "Oh."

"I'd like to stay, really. Besides, he goes up to bed in a little while, doesn't he?"

"I do not," Nicholas said. He lifted his fair head, glared long and hard at his mother, and put his face down close to his coloring book again; there was a little sound he made, a kind of grunt of seriousness, whenever he began to color. Kyra frowned at her son. It hurt her that he now had that English schoolboy complexion, that chilled, sensitive, pre-cold look about the nostrils and eyelids. Sensing this critical appraisal, he gave an upward, angelic smile. One front tooth was perhaps a millimeter shorter than the other. Kyra slid from her chair, coat and all, and lay down over her son. She covered the back of his head, that fine child's hair, in England more brown than blond, with kisses.

"Kyra, come on," Charlie said. He was embarrassed that she'd done it in front of Brian.

She pulled the black coat's sides into wings and hid herself, and Nicholas below her, completely. Nicholas giggled. "You're tenting me," he said. She sat up and pretended to smooth his hair. "I can't always resist him," she said to her husband, and he said, "Yes, but now your hair."

"What about my hair?"

"You go and look, and if it takes twenty minutes—"

"You'll what?" She walked to him on her knees, causing Nicholas behind her to laugh. "You will do exactly what?" she flirted, cocking her head to the side, kneeling between his nice pin-striped knees. She was aware of Brian's gaze on her back, on the back of her black Japanese coat.

"I can't stand walking into people's houses late," Charlie said. "It makes me feel like a puppet or something."

"My hair is supposed to be uneven," she said. "You didn't notice, puppet."

He rose, relieved. "Look, Brian, if you want another drink or anything, please don't hesitate, but I think you already know that."

"Sure."

"He can't stay here," Nicholas said. He pointed a crayon at Brian. Then Brian made a small, really almost trivial mistake. He winked at Nicholas. Nicholas screamed as if he'd been shot. "He can't, he can't!" Nicholas shouted. "You can't leave me!" He made a run for his mother, who was still on the floor, and caught her, burying his face in her coat.

"Knock, knock," Kyra said, knuckles rapping the light-brown head. "It sounds hollow to me, baby. Nobody home."

"I have to get out of here," Charlie said.

"Please do," Brian said. "I'm sure he'll settle down, given a moment or two," meaning, "after you're out the door."

"He needs a bath," Kyra said, standing.

"A bath," Charlie said, awed at what Brian was up against, fearing he would change his mind.

"A bath," Brian said; he nodded.

In the doorway Kyra turned back and whispered swiftly, "If he gets very bad, he likes being lifted." Brian shook his head, puzzled, until Kyra's hands shaped air. "Up," she said. "I don't know why it works, but it does."

To end the storm of emotion, Brian held Nicholas on his shoulder at the window so that they could watch his parents disappear into a black taxi whose windshield wipers clocked back and forth, though it was scarcely drizzling. Brian thought he could feel everything Nicholas was feeling. For a moment it wasn't like watching a friend, and the friend's wife, leave; it was like watching his own parents forgetting his existence and going off to a strange house, to a faraway party, at night.

⟨ The bath: Nicholas's face was surly under the cloth. Brian washed his ears and the corners of his mouth with grave gentleness. Nicholas turned around and presented small shoulder blades. He finished washing himself with his back to Brian. Brian gathered him into a towel, and Nicholas gazed at him, hooded and shivering. Still kneeling, Brian scrubbed each arm and then his chest with the towel, and to his surprise Nicholas leaned into him, into his arms, to be scrubbed more firmly, and Brian smelled wet child.

In the sitting room he read aloud, with Nicholas lying heavily across his lap and turning the pages. Nicholas surprised him again—he was in his pajamas, but his feet were bare, and when Brian let go of the book, he thrust his bare feet into Brian's hands to warm them. The heels had a grittiness, and when Brian ran his thumb across them, the toes flexed.

"Now a story with you in it," Nicholas demanded, closing the book.

Brian didn't know what to make of his life for a four-year-old, yet he was determined to find a bit of himself, his past, that could charm this bright child, so he began, "Well, once when I was your age," and was interrupted.

"You were not my age."

"I was, once."

"You were not."

35

It was a puzzle. He tried a way out. "Once when I was a little boy, and I was already in school, I went over the wall."

It worked. "What wall?"

"The wall around the schoolyard. I escaped. The doctor was supposed to come and look at us that day, and the way I had understood it my mother was going to be with me during the examination. It was going to be the first time I was ever looked at by a doctor, and I guess I was frightened about him seeing me alone and finding something wrong. When she didn't turn up, I went up over the wall and home." He remembered her startled laugh.

"That's the story?"

"Once, too, I fell in love with an older woman." He mused. "I was five and she was six. I caught her in the cloakroom and kissed her. Her name was Beryl. Then, when she grew up, she was my older sister's best friend, and I had to see her all the time, though I no longer loved her. Served me right." Served him right, too, that the small bare feet untucked themselves from his hand.

"That's not a story," Nicholas said. "Not."

"It's all you get." Brian shouldered him up the stairs to his room, Nicholas patting the ceiling as they went, pleased because he had never touched that ceiling before. His small room had an artfulness—Kyra's sense of the way a little boy's room ought to look—but Nicholas was at war with this artfulness, and he was winning. As Brian went to turn off the light, Nicholas said, "Scratch," and rolled over onto his stomach. Brian leaned forward, scratching between shoulder blades so small he smiled, against his fingertips the delicious cottony heat of pajamas. A pair of stockings was crumpled on the floor by the bed, and Brian saw Kyra pausing in the doorway, seeing that her son's exuberant messiness had again defeated her ambitions, and, shrugging, beginning to pick up toys; then pausing on the bed's edge to peel off her stockings, which she airily discards in a gesture of—what? Alliance with that exuberance. Brian stopped scratching. "That's all," he said. "Night now."

"I know," Nicholas said.

When Brian started to pull the door closed, Nicholas whispered, "Leave it so I can hear you."

⟨ Though the lowest panes of the sitting room's narrow old ⟨ windows were smoked white by radiators, high up the cold black glass showed the silver-foil patterns of frost. At the corner of the rug, the cat sat and squared its shoulders, making itself slim as a bottle to stare at the stranger. From Charlie's armchair, Brian could hear the tiny catch as, at last, the cat yawned. He watched the cat melt around chair legs, out of the room, and fell asleep.

He woke with the sense of having been shocked out of a light sleep; it was a shock that could have stemmed either from something dreamed or something real, and at first he thought dreamed, because he had been kissing Charlie's wife—a rain of urgent kisses on her eyelids, the corners of her mouth, under her tilted jaw. Guilt came at him sharply, but something else had happened too, something in the room. A slow falling dapple of lights on the ceiling meant a taxi in the freezing street outside. He listened for the latch, sure it was still too early, but the sound he heard was from upstairs, a hard, halting scream. He took the steep stairs three at a time, and there was Nicholas, in the wedge of light thrown in from the doorway, crouching against the wall in a tangle of covers.

"What is it?" Brian said. "What?"

Nicholas wouldn't answer. He moved so that his back was hard against the wall. His hair was darkened from dream sweat.

"Nicholas, come on, what was it? What's the matter?"

"You hit me." Fiercely.

37

"What?"

"You hit me." He slid his back up against the wall until he was on his feet, bedclothes around his ankles, his pupils shrinking in the light.

"You dreamed something hurt you?"

"You did."

All at once Brian imagined Kyra's disbelief, her pure face turning to his as if he were something too terrible to be understood. And he saw Charlie, dark with fury, turning not on Brian but on Kyra: This was your fault. You're the one who decided to trust him with our son.

"I can't have hit you, Nicholas," he said reasonably, though his voice sounded strange to him, too desperately pitched to reassure. His voice, he knew, was full of guilt. "I've been downstairs, haven't I—I've been reading, and I fell asleep myself. I have not been in your room."

Nicholas said in torment, "You were in here."

Brian couldn't think. Surprising himself, he grabbed Nicholas by the shoulders and lofted him from the bed into the air, the boy's pajama top bellying out and his hair tipped into his eyes. "It was you!" Nicholas kicked, narrowly missing Brian's cheek, so that Brian could not check a little hiss of anger. "It was, you hit me, it was, you hit me!"

"I did not. You were asleep," Brian said, lifting him higher, evenly returning that furious downward stare until he knew by some subtle change in the child's eyes that he was believed. A tear pelted Brian's upper lip, and he licked it away. Nicholas's breaths came in raw gusts, socking down to the diaphragm like hiccups, as Brian began to turn slowly, carefully, his arms beginning to shake, turning faster and faster on the rug until the boy laughed, and that was how they were when Kyra stood in the doorway, her face very clear from the cold. "And what is this?" she said.

"All through now?" Brian asked. When Nicholas nodded

he was lowered to the bed. He bounced twice, then scooted under the covers, dragging them up to his chest. Kyra sat down, near enough for Brian to feel the cold air on her coat. She stroked Nicholas's forehead, laying her palm against that infinitely fresh, wild, superheated quality of a child's skin after tears, and she coaxed, "So were you good?"

"No," he said, and caught his breath.

"You weren't good for Brian? How?"

"I was scared of him."

"He had a real nightmare," Brian said. "And I guess I was in it, somehow. It seems to have scared him pretty badly."

"That was a dream," she said to Nicholas, "this is real," and with a finger deftly cleaned the sleep from his eyes, glancing up to find Brian regarding her with what was clearly, unmistakably love.

"Are you happy?" Brian said.

"Happy?" she said. "Yes, I am"—shocked to find her own happiness, always so hard to pin down, so easy to read in his face.

No One's a Mystery

For my eighteenth birthday Jack gave me a five-year diary with a latch and a little key, light as a dime. I was sitting beside him scratching at the lock, which didn't want to work, when he thought he saw his wife's Cadillac in the distance, coming toward us. He pushed me down onto the dirty floor of the pickup and kept one hand on my head while I inhaled the musk of his cigarettes in the dashboard ashtray and sang along with Rosanne Cash on the tape deck. We'd been drinking tequila and the bottle was between his legs, resting up against his crotch, where the seam of his Levi's was bleached linen-white, though the Levi's were nearly new. I don't know why his Levi's always bleached like that, along the seams and at the knees. In a curve of cloth his zipper glinted, gold.

"It's her," he said. "She keeps the lights on in the daytime. I can't think of a single habit in a woman that irritates me more than that." When he saw that I was going to stay still he took his hand from my head and ran it through his own dark hair.

"Why does she?" I said.

"She thinks it's safer. Why does she need to be safer? She's driving exactly fifty-five miles an hour. She believes in those signs: 'Speed Monitored by Aircraft.' It doesn't matter that you can look up and see that the sky is empty."

"She'll see your lips move, Jack. She'll know you're talking to someone."

"She'll think I'm singing along with the radio."

He didn't lift his hand, just raised the fingers in salute while the pressure of his palm steadied the wheel, and I heard the Cadillac honk twice, musically; he was driving easily eighty miles an hour. I studied his boots. The elk heads stitched into the leather were bearded with frayed thread, the toes were scuffed, and there was a compact wedge of muddy manure between the heel and the sole—the same boots he'd been wearing for the two years I'd known him. On the tape deck Rosanne Cash sang, "Nobody's into me, no one's a mystery."

"Do you think she's getting famous because of who her daddy is or for herself?" Jack said.

"There are about a hundred pop tops on the floor, did you know that? Some little kid could cut a bare foot on one of these, Jack."

"No little kids get into this truck except for you."

"How come you let it get so dirty?"

" 'How come,' " he mocked. "You even sound like a kid. You can get back into the seat now, if you want. She's not going to look over her shoulder and see you."

"How do you know?"

"I just know," he said. "Like I know I'm going to get meat loaf for supper. It's in the air. Like I know what you'll be writing in that diary."

"What will I be writing?" I knelt on my side of the seat and craned around to look at the butterfly of dust printed on my jeans. Outside the window Wyoming was dazzling in the heat. The wheat was fawn and yellow and parted smoothly by the thin dirt road. I could smell the water in the irrigation ditches hidden in the wheat.

"Tonight you'll write, 'I love Jack. This is my birthday present from him. I can't imagine anybody loving anybody more than I love Jack.'"

"I can't."

"In a year you'll write, 'I wonder what I ever really saw in Jack. I wonder why I spent so many days just riding around in his pickup. It's true he taught me something about sex. It's true there wasn't ever much else to do in Cheyenne.'"

"I won't write that."

"In two years you'll write, 'I wonder what that old guy's name was, the one with the curly hair and the filthy dirty pickup truck and time on his hands.'"

"I won't write that."

"No?"

"Tonight I'll write, 'I love Jack. This is my birthday present from him. I can't imagine anybody loving anybody more than I love Jack.'"

"No, you can't," he says. "You can't imagine it."

"In a year I'll write, 'Jack should be home any minute now. The table's set—my grandmother's linen and her old silver and the yellow candles left over from the wedding—but I don't know if I can wait until after the trout *à la Navarra* to make love to him.'"

"It must have been a fast divorce."

"In two years I'll write, 'Jack should be home by now. Little Jack is hungry for his supper. He said his first word today besides "Mama" and "Papa." He said, "Caca."'"

Jack laughed. "He was probably trying to fingerpaint with caca on the bathroom wall when you heard him say it."

"In three years I'll write, 'My nipples are a little sore from nursing Eliza Rosamund.'"

"Rosamund. Every little girl should have a middle name she hates."

" 'Her breath smells like vanilla and her eyes are just Jack's color of blue.' "

"That's nice," Jack said.

"So? Which one do you like?"

"I like yours," he said. "But I believe mine."

"It doesn't matter. I believe mine."

"Not in your heart of hearts, you don't."

"You're wrong."

"I'm not wrong," he said. "And her breath would smell like your milk, and it's kind of a bittersweet smell, if you want to know the truth."

Two
Ghosts
of Us

I left Carl and went to live in a Sombrillo Court Garden apartment, not because I liked them so much but because you could always rent one right away. Mrs. Vigil had a habit of running both forefingers from her earlobes along either side of her jaw and bringing them together in a steeple that rested on her chin; she made this gesture, squinted across the steeple at my black eye, and asked for fifty dollars' damage deposit. On the television by the cash register, Jane Fonda's *Workout* tape was playing. Jane Fonda was lying on her side, and her leg rose straight until the knee was wedged against her hollow cheek, her toes pointed. Mrs. Vigil sighed, a deep sigh—disappointment in the world, and in me. She'd known me since I was little, and I'd been her son Jamie Lee's girl friend in high school; I think she thought we'd marry.

"There's some ice for that eye in the back," Mrs. Vigil said; she meant she'd go and get it. In the back was where she lived.

"It's had ice," I said. "It's resting to start hurting again."

"Carl isn't going to be coming around, is he? I can't have fighting."

Carl was my husband; I shook my head softly to show I was against him, too. "If he comes, you can call the police."

"The pleece hate domestics," she said. "You know how long it would take them. You know as well as I."

"He doesn't know where I went, Mrs. Vigil."

She stayed doubtful.

"He doesn't, he doesn't know."

"How many places could you go?" was her logical question. I rested two knuckles gingerly against my brow bone in preparation for it, but it never came; instead, she gave me the key.

Jamie Lee Vigil watched me go toward the apartment with a duffel bag over my shoulder and the six-pack of Coors Lite I had bought at the Pojoaque 7-Eleven. He was settling a baby deer into place below a plaster doe in the courtyard, surrounded by paper Mexican flowers and real, leaning hollyhocks, and the Madonna statue Mrs. Vigil insisted watched over the place. I held the six-pack by the white plastic web that bound the cans together, bouncing nicely from my middle finger, a spot of cold against my left leg while I fretted the key in the old lock. There was a rusty brass number 5 on the hollow-core door. I opened it and went through the bare apartment, breathing air that had collected the smell of sun-heated old paint, dropping the duffel in a corner. Then I sat down on it, popped a beer, and drank from the tear-drop opening, so crisp in that dewy, somehow mild-feeling metal. I had my first moment of believing I was separate from Carl. I thought of the cheap wicker furniture I could buy and the flickery old black-and-white TV I would have and how I would never wake up to Carl's favorite television evangelist again. No more Sunday mornings ruined by *Hallelujah*s.

I went to the door with a can for Jamie Lee, holding it up to see if he wanted it; going by me in the doorway, he said, "Wow," about my eye. I took the duffel again, and he lay down in the middle of the floor, balancing the beer on his chest right above where his heart would be, under his sweaty cotton T-shirt. I told him what I'd observed, that there wasn't fifty dollars' worth of damage I could do to this place, and he laughed and said if that's what his mother wanted, she must have thought I'd be trouble. Jamie Lee smelled fine to me, alone in that hot apartment. It has always mattered to me the way men smell. I can't sleep with a man if he smells wrong, and it's not at all predictable, who will and who won't. The traffic on the Taos highway went by steadily. There had been lots of tourists all summer long, and summer wasn't over, though my car was the single one in front of the Sombrillo Court Garden Apartments. In summer sometimes, listening to other people's cars going somewhere when you are staying very still is as nice as half-listening to a river. Jamie Lee squinted up at me and said he hadn't remembered my legs being so long and I said, "I guess."

"You know that joke? Legs all the way up to her ass?"

"We've known each other since first grade, haven't we, Jamie Lee?"

"All the way up to her *ass*." He left a little silence in case I suddenly happened to get it. "First grade, uh-huh, Mrs. Stephano, the Mormon, and everybody making those jokes about her not being her husband's only wife. I've always remembered something she told us. It seems funny to have remembered something that long, don't it? First grade was a long time ago. A lot has happened since first grade."

"What was it?" I was leaning forward, picking at a scab on my knee. His nipples made sweet brown shapes below the sticky T-shirt and the thumping of his heart moved the beer can a little up and down.

"She said in your entire life you're lucky if you can count five friends, five real friends, for yourself. Could you ever count five friends?" I shook my head, no. "Either could I," Jamie Lee said. "It's weird, but if I was trying to count the five I would always have counted you."

"It's not so weird, Jamie Lee," I said. "Once you feel some things, you never unfeel them. I would have counted you."

"Scary, huh?" he said contentedly. "It's like when we were inseparable, even though I haven't seen you since you got married. Isn't it funny we never run into each other? Much less be alone in the same room."

"Do you like it?"

"Don't ask me questions like that."

"Listen, Jamie Lee. I just left my husband and I'm kind of in a mood to ask any question I want, and it doesn't matter to me who likes it or not. It doesn't have to matter to me right now."

"Let's not fight," he said. "All I do is fight with somebody or other lately, but not ever with you before, so let's not."

In a way, not a lot had happened to Jamie Lee since first grade. He took over the Sombrillo Court after his father's coronary, and now he was essentially his mother's right arm, though he had his own apartment, an upstairs one, I thought. "Fine," I said. "We're not going to." Somebody or other: his mother.

"What do you want to do instead?" He could tell that I liked him grinning up at me from my brand-new-rented floor, so he came and put his chin on my knee and began to slide the flat of his hand up along the seam of my shorts, along into my crotch and down the seam on the other leg, like a little kid who invents some game on the spur of the moment—you can't move your hand on her except along that line. In my crotch the seam was frayed and his hand felt delicious there and I could feel the coppery heat of the zipper through the soft cloth when he held his hand against it. I slid down from the duffel bag onto the bare floor and the old hardwood was nice against my back. I tugged Jamie Lee's T-shirt over his head—he lifted his arms like a little boy, and for a moment his face was oddly shrouded in the damp, binding cloth, and then it pulled away leaving his even grin and his dark mustache and his eyes, looking into mine quite straight, which I liked because I could almost have come from that look.

He worked my left boot off, so that my foot was suddenly naked and light, and he laid my foot along his jaw for a moment, just holding it there.

He drew my other boot off, and I lifted my rear end from the floor so that he could slide my shorts down, because if you make love in the back seat of a car, there's a certain kind of cooperation you learn, and it's like riding a bicycle, knowledge new-minted and complete as soon as you need it, and pleasing because you didn't have to piece it together like other things salvaged from the past. It was nice, being undressed, it made me feel there was a chance everything else might be taken care of. My pubic hair was matted down into the cleft, and Jamie Lee ran his fingers through it to make it spike against his cheek, locked, tiny curls the color of his five o'clock shadow, which made the whites of his eyes seem whiter. Once in high school we were talking about ways of dying, and I said I wanted to be eaten by a tiger, and he told me I was crazy, that it would hurt like hell, that the way to die was by falling, because your heart would stop of itself before you hit the ground. I strained against him and imagined a golden face between my legs, and in truth down there I felt grainy and vivid, a flushed softness about to be torn from the bone, his jaw working quietly, his teeth below his lips, his eyes closed.

I came and he held very still, as if he didn't want to frighten me out of it, and he couldn't tell, probably, that he couldn't have.

Then he slid into me before I had a chance to collect my wits, and we were scooting across the floor, my ass making little cricket chirps on the polished wood, though it didn't hurt.

As long as he was in me, I wanted to make Jamie Lee happy for the rest of his life. He was so urgent with want, my body could've done it, too—I had that sensation of goodness which comes of being all someone wants. He said, "Dar—," close to my ear, the beer slapping against the walls of my stomach, and then, "—ling, dar—," and I could feel the pulse in my throat and the sweatiness of my chest and the straining flutter that meant I was about to come again with him, and he said, "—ling, *oh* no," and withdrew just before he came, and there was the funny pearly dollop on my stomach, below the navel, and he seemed a little embarrassed to keep coming for such a long time, as if it looked like he was desperate.

"I didn't know if you had any other protection," he said. It had made him shy.

"I didn't," I said. "Thank you."

"I know you," he said. "You know, you're still so nice-looking, even with that eye," and I flinched my face away before he could touch it. I didn't feel nice, I felt a sort of post-coital messiness and sadness taking over, so I got up and walked into the little bathroom. I washed myself and studied my eye in the mirror and the greatest thing I felt at that moment was a longing to be alone, but that didn't reflect on Jamie Lee, I guessed. It didn't really have anything to do with who he was. It was just a lonely feeling that descended. I put my arms around myself and rocked myself for a minute.

He had his Levi's on when I came out and that seemed sensitive of him, and he went in and closed the door and I heard the seat of the toilet go up with that porcelain-wood clap that always greets a man about to pee, and then there was something at the door, the front door of the apartment, landing hard about where the rusty number 5 was, not really urgent, not really knocking, but not about to be ignored, either. I stepped back so that I couldn't be seen through the front window, and glanced down at my jeans and Jamie Lee's fertile, rank-sweet male T-shirt twisted together on the floor, and it was like looking down at two ghosts of us. I could hear Jamie Lee aiming into the toilet with a little muted, pleasurable, entirely unselfconscious whistling, not knowing there was anything wrong.

I whispered, "You go to hell, Carl," to get my voice, and then I yelled it. "You go to hell, Carl," and he said "No," in a stubborn way, just "No." So, stubbornly, I said, "Get the fuck away from here, can't you?" and he said "No" again, and Jamie Lee in the bathroom grew more still and maybe fearful, shaking the last few drops from himself, and I said, "Can't you leave me alone? Can't you?"

Carl said, "No."

"If you go away," I said, "I'll call you tomorrow, I will, and we can talk about it, is that a deal?"

"No, it's not."

I said, "What, then?"

"You let me in."

"Carl, if you don't leave, it's going to be over."

This must have had finality, because he said, "I'll go away on one condition. That you tell me you'll come home tomorrow."

"I can't tell you that." It occurred to me that if I said it, I was going to hurt Jamie Lee's feelings.

"Can't or won't?"

"If I did say it, even I wouldn't know if it was true."

"You say it, O.K., and it is true, or this door between us comes down." The door rattled in its frame for proof.

He would have done it, too, so I said, "I'll come home if you go away on the count of three. With no more shit."

"That's reasonable."

"One."

"We both need a while to think, is that it?"

"Two."

"A night apart to cool out, is that what you're thinking?"

I could tell from his voice that he wanted to see me so badly it was all he could do to keep it to himself. "Three."

"Hey," he said.

"Hey what?"

He whispered it so that I could hardly hear.

"Three," I said again. I felt the blindest blind hatred of him.

He whispered it again. His lips must have been right against that hollow core. "I love you," he said, clearly enough so that even Jamie Lee, still in the bathroom, could hear.

"If you ever, ever hurt me again," I said carefully, "I mean just once, even by accident, if you even come close, if I even see from your face that you're thinking about it, I'm leaving, I mean I am really leaving you, I'm going to go so far away you'll never hear another word about me. I'll do it so that nobody knows where I am to tell you. You know I can do it that way. If I even once see from your face that you're thinking about lifting your hand."

"I know," he said. "I know you will."

"Your fucking hand."

"I know."

"You hurt my *face*."

"I know. I know I did. And you're beautiful."

"And you suck." I felt as if my head was very clear. "I counted sucking three. I want you to leave right now."

"That doesn't count as shit," he said. "When I said I love you. That was true."

He rattled the door again, very very lightly, and let go. Then he climbed back into his pickup, gunning the engine. I went, covering myself with my shirt but not buttoning it, to crouch down on my heels at the window and watch him. He was combing his hair in the rearview mirror, palming the back of his head. Then he hit his horn twice in farewell and pulled out into the traffic on the highway, and Jamie Lee came up behind me and squatted to be at my level, and I smelled the sweet wet smell of his skin. He'd washed his face while he was in there, having to listen. When we were in high school and he played shortstop, he smelled like that. Suddenly I remembered what it was like to be alone in the bleachers after a game, waiting for him to finish showering, the summer moon coming up across the empty diamond. I said, "Thank you for being so quiet in there," and he shook his head at me.

"You don't have to go, you know. He can't make you."

"You might not understand this, but he doesn't have to make me go. I'm just going."

"You're going because you're really frightened of what he'll do if you don't. I can see that. What I'm saying is that you can stay here for as long as you want, and he can't lay a finger on you. I'll make sure."

"That's not it."

"You can't want to go back to him. I don't believe it. Not after this."

It took me a minute to understand that his *this* was the way we had made love, that that was still for him the overwhelming thing that had happened that afternoon. We were kneeling below the window, our heads out of sight from the highway, and I felt the light, pleasant sweat that sometimes follows a fear. I kissed Jamie Lee out of delight at having found him again, and because the depth of his misunderstanding frightened me a little, but he stopped the kiss. "I get it," he said. "You used me. I was a good way of getting even."

"I didn't use you, Jamie Lee. That was the last thing I did."

"Years go by, years, without a word from you, and it begins to make a kind of sense, you're gone, and see, it's just the way things worked out, that you married somebody else, not me.

Then all of a sudden, one day, there you just are, and it's as if I never forgot a thing."

"Tell me you hated it," I said.

"I hated it," Jamie Lee said, his first lie to me ever.

That left me with the funniest feeling, as if I had nowhere left to go, but of course I did go—home.

Sweet Disposition

The house was set very prettily against its bluff; all morning the mist spilled down the bluff, around the house's corners, and into the arroyo, where it hid all but the pale cane handles that were the heads of foxtails. This mist carried with it something of the benevolent quality of new-fallen snow. Jenny had never seen anything like it. For once, Delgado's dogs, which slept in the abandoned cars in the junkyard on the far side of the arroyo, didn't fight; neither did Jenny and Sam, who had been at odds for a month. That morning, when Jenny ran down the road and stopped before the sorrel horse, his rough winter coat was steaming in tufts and curls. As she neared the fence, his ears tipped forward—first the left ear, always the more alert, then the languorous right.

She was careful about touching him, though he was beautiful. The deep inverted commas of his nostrils, furled at the upper ends, perfectly mimicked the shape of his ears, whose tips hooked inward, almost touching above his coarse forelock. His eyes were dark, the lashes deerlike. She remembered to keep her hand flat so that he would not be confused about where her fingers were. She held out the apple. His nose dipped to her hand, and his breath, rising in white strokes, joined the cloud of Jenny's breath. She liked that, and yawned to make more breath, but once he had the apple he swung his head away.

She stamped her feet to warm them. It had been winter since October, and it wasn't Christmas yet. When Jenny felt claustrophobic, and that was often, she went running. After the first week, when she passed his stretch of fence the horse—who belonged to Jenny and Sam's downhill neighbors, the Gallardos—had lifted his head and neighed, and after that he neighed each time he saw her. She began to bring him apples and crusts of bread, thinking the Gallardos wouldn't mind, but not troubling to ask them, either. Now when she started down the road from her house, the horse would canter across the snowy field to the corner of fence where they met. She was something in his day, and he was something in hers. Yet she tried not to presume; she still approached him with caution, because Sam said he had once kicked a dog's skull in, and he had the nervy head-tossing mannerisms of horses who are never ridden. Even now she sometimes scared him—wariness would overcome him at some innocent, too sudden gesture of hers, and he would shy away and run. This never failed to wound her. The next morning at the fence corner, his nose would gust in butterfly pulses, fusing trust and evasion, across her extended palm, and she would feel forgiven.

Sam often wished that, out of courtesy, Jenny had consulted Socorro Gallardo—the sorrel belonged to Socorro's husband, Juan, but he was often away. Jenny didn't understand how binding courtesy could be in small neighborhoods, how glaring its omission. You couldn't make Jenny talk to Socorro, though, or Socorro acknowledge Jenny's existence unless she had to; one of those mysterious dislikes that sometimes seemed to separate pretty women had settled between them, Sam had no idea why. He couldn't afford to discourage Jenny from feeding the horse, because it was one of the few things she seemed genuinely to like about living in the country, and Sam was counting on a gradual accrual of details, the steady accumulation of habit, to help Jenny settle down. The house had been his idea first, and it had somehow refused to become Jenny's house at all. Once or twice she'd said she wished they had looked harder for something in Santa Fe; once or twice he'd thought she was inventing reasons to go into town more often than was strictly necessary; once, just once, she had disappeared for groceries and come back without so much as a carton of milk. What would it take to make Jenny feel at home? This morning Sam had tried a lecture, though his lectures were rarely successful. Remember the way everyone had told them stories about how buying a house would break up some couple who had been rock-solid for years? Remember how everyone had delighted in telling them such stories? How Jenny had sworn it would never, never happen to them?

"How can I forget?" Jenny said. She left him alone with this unsatisfying answer, and in baggy pants and layers of ragged sweaters ran down the raw dirt road to the corner where the sorrel horse waited, his chin on the fence post.

Sam rested his forehead against the cold window and watched his wife. He'd done the kitchen in quarry tile and costly stainless steel, everything he thought she wanted. He'd done the bedroom in a shade of russet she had happened to admire in the paint store, though he was only lukewarm about it, and when she told him she liked high tech in bathrooms he hadn't fought too hard, though he had coveted a claw-footed old caldron of a tub he had come across in a secondhand shop. So what would it take, what would it finally require, to make Jenny happy? Or was she happy now, this instant? She had an almost wild horse eating out of her hand.

{ After Christmas it turned so cold that Old Man Sandoval, who lived down the road, hated to come out of his house, so Sam walked the half mile to the row of mailboxes, starred with mud, to collect the old man's mail: samples of soap, a circular from a state senator, the bill from the community well. One windy morning, Socorro caught Sam on the road after he'd dropped off Sandoval's mail and she asked him in for coffee. He couldn't think of a polite way to refuse; then he decided he didn't want to think of a way. Socorro had three sons. Two were nowhere in sight, but the youngest stared at Sam from a corner of the kitchen until Socorro made him sit at the table and warned him to be good. When her back was turned, the boy edged his way around to Sam and began dropping M&Ms into his coffee, feeding them in one at a time, as if they were dangerous pills. He looked up hopefully to see if Sam was disgusted; Sam made a terrible face. The boy returned to his chair. Socorro, her back to them, was singing at the stove. She interrupted herself to tell Sam, "I really like what you're doing to the house, you know? It's so different than it was."

"It's going to turn out all right," Sam said modestly.

"Oh, no—beautiful. It's going to turn out beautiful. I thought nothing very good could happen to that house."

"You didn't like it?"

"Oh, I liked it." She looked over her shoulder, unwilling to hurt his feelings. Two elderly Spanish women, distant cousins of hers, had sold the house to Jenny and Sam last fall, and before it was sold Socorro had been inside it often, retrieving her sons, whom the cousins spoiled with ice cream and daytime television. "But it was always, you know, so dark inside."

"It isn't now. I tore out a wall. That opened it up." He lifted his hands from his coffee cup in a sweeping gesture meant to indicate light. If it wasn't for Jenny, he would ask Socorro to come up and see for herself; they were both aware of this, and skirted it delicately.

"You did? I saw all of that dirt going out." She laughed, as if that were a wonderful thing to have done, to have trundled a wall, wheelbarrow by wheelbarrow, out the door and dumped it down the arroyo. So she'd been watching. "Such a lot of time you've put into it," she said. "Juan doesn't like to do things with his hands, not unless it's to engines."

Her little boy slipped from his chair and went to the refrigerator. He peeled a slice of baloney from its wrapper, screwed it into a cone, fed several M&Ms into the cone, and ate it.

"Juan only likes to spend all day working on his cars. He never really wants to go anywhere."

On Saturdays, Sam had often observed Juan flat on his back in the gloom below a rusted Mustang while his youngest son squatted nearby, waiting for the impatient prodding of a dirty sneaker toe, the upward shift of a knee, that signaled a need: for a smaller wrench, a rag, a cold Coke from the house. Music from the car's radio bound father and son more closely than conversation. The car was an island, and they had been stranded there to make the best of it. Its underside was a shadowy realm of spider gears, exhaust pipes, bell housing, muffler, and struts. Sam felt an absurd urge to defend her husband to Socorro—to prove to her, somehow, what a fine thing it was to fix a car with your son watching. "But he's really great with engines. Everyone says he can tell what's wrong just by listening. I've been thinking my pickup needs a little work."

She gave in right away, or seemed to. "Oh, he is. He's very good at what he likes. You all are."

All men, he guessed she meant, and felt flattered, as if her recognition of male stubbornness was a kind of approval in which he was included.

"When anything else goes wrong, though, he hates it if I ask him to fix it. Jenny's lucky that what you like is houses."

She said "Jenny" lightly, apprehensively, looking over her shoulder again, as if again she might offend, and for the first time Sam noticed a nick, a tiny hooked scar, at the corner of Socorro's eye. Her cheek was downy against the fall of her hair.

"What happened to your eye?"

"Nothing." She was startled.

"Right here." He touched the corner of his own eye.

"No, nothing."

They looked away from each other. "I forgot what I was doing," she said. She turned a singeing tortilla.

Her little boy came up and laid a slice of baloney on Sam's knee. Sam unstuck it from his knee and ate it in two bites. He had forgotten the cold taste of baloney. "Who are you *really*?" the boy demanded.

Socorro knelt, zipped his snowsuit, carried him kicking into the living room, flung open the front door, and set him down. "You know who he is," she said. "Now go find your brothers."

"I don't know where to look."

"You tell your brothers I said to take care of you. If I find out different, you're in trouble—all three, no matter who started it first. No getting in fights. No going near the ditch. No going as far as the road."

"I said I don't know where to look."

"I've got to go too," Sam said.

"You do?" She sounded sorry she had opened the door. "No breakfast?"

"Work," Sam said. "Got to." He had adopted her apologetic tone—so closely, in fact, that for a moment he sounded to himself as if he were mocking her. Suddenly worried that she would misinterpret, he made his next sentence deliberately, self-consciously rueful, using a true Jenny tactic, presenting something he believed as a fragment of farce. "In dreams begin responsibilities, huh? I'm late."

She looked down at her unmoving son, whose small legs

were braced wide apart. She laid a hand at the back of his head and pushed. "You go, idiot," she said. "Look where you always look."

⟨ The horse had no shelter. He slept in falling snow, one hind
⟨ leg cocked. His manger was a fender from a Volkswagen, and each evening Socorro waded through snow to pour the feed into the fender, lifting the heavy bag to her shoulder and steadying it while the golden, dusty stuff shuttled through the sharp air. The horse ignored Socorro, waiting until she had turned her back before plunging his nose into the grain. Jenny was pleased with the distance the horse kept between himself and Socorro. She interpreted it to mean that the sorrel wished the one who was feeding him was Jenny.

Just how much would Juan want for the horse? Was his state of neglect a sign that he would come cheap? His flaxen mane was encrusted with burrs the size of cloves; even the star on his forehead was dirty, and one of his knees had a cruel black callus. Sam had told her the horse had been ruined somehow, but how? Now no one, not even Juan, really liked to handle him. Jenny would lean on the fence and daydream. Sorrel hairs like slivers were embedded in the grain of the gray fence rail: this was the corner where he leaned to wait for her. A hundred dollars? Two hundred? Five? Oats? Boarding? Vet bills? Why should she want a horse she knew she could never ride? That was a good question—so good, in fact, that she heard it in Sam's voice. She'd never even seen the sorrel with a halter on. Who knew if she could handle him? Why not find a quarter-horse mare with a glossy coat and a sweet disposition? What should she offer Juan in order not to insult him but not to be taken advantage of, either? It was impossible.

Impossible. The long whiskers bent to allow the plush nose to fit more closely into Jenny's cupped hand. Though it was the dead of winter, his breath smelled grassy. She had forgotten to bring an apple. He was doing it for love.

⟨⟨ After New Year's, the reef of ice in the irrigation ditch began to corrode and fall away, its edges thinning into sheets frail and dark as mica that extended far out over the water, except under the bridge, where the blue day-long shadow protected a pristine drift. Over coffee early one morning, Jenny watched the two older Gallardo boys dragging a sled up the bluff; the smallest boy followed, eating some snow. He wore only one mitten. At the crest there was a scuffle that ended in one of the older boys' holding the smallest while the third brother bucked down through dirty patches of snow, forcing himself to fall off at the bottom, somersault several times in slow motion, stop, somersault again—narrowly missing a juniper trunk—jump to his feet, deal a number of mortal blows to an invisible enemy, and finally climb the slope again, the sled sawing behind him on its frayed rope. At the top he caught the smallest boy and held him while the other brother lay on his belly on the sled and pushed off. He had to tip the sled nearly vertical to get it going. The little boy battered his brother's chest with his square brown head until his brother scooped up a handful of snow and washed the smallest boy's face with it. He was the only one she liked, Jenny decided. She remembered how the bone in your chin hurt when your face was washed with snow.

When most of the snow had been scraped away, exposing the wet earth of the bluff, the youngest boy finally got a turn. He fell off the sled at the bottom, somersaulted violently, jumped up, parried the blows of his attackers until, his face going through heroic contortions, he was exhausted. Only then did he let his guard down, was shot through the heart, reeled backward and died, scuffing up a lot of snow in his death agonies, but by that time Jenny was his only audience, for the top of the bluff was bare.

"No fair," Jenny said softly, to herself.

That night she woke in moonlight to find the wood stove had gone out. She had been dreaming of the sorrel horse. In the dream she was supposed to trim his hooves—ugly work, and difficult, trying to file those petrified tatters of bone into proper ovals. She was crouched, facing away from him, with a hoof tipped up between her knees, his tail fanning down her back with that starched whisper peculiar to horsehair, and as she cupped his hoof, which he was letting her hold lightly—being, for once, in a mood of gentle trust—Jenny could see, within the caldera of cracked hoof, a tiny emerald-green frog blinking back at her.

The wind was beating against the panes of the window high above Sam's shoulder, and he had taken most of the quilts. "The stove's out," she said.

"You get it," he said. "I'm asleep."

"You're the only one it likes."

"It's not alive, Jen."

"It hates me."

"You think everyone hates you. Even Socorro."

"Why did you think of Socorro?" No answer. "Have you been flirting with her, Sam?" Very gently: "You shouldn't, you know. Because they're Spanish. You can't tell how she'd take it. You can't tell how he would."

He woke enough to turn wary. "You're right. I can't tell how she'd take a thing that never happened."

"I've *seen* you." This wasn't true, but she waited to see if a glimmer of guilt would flaw his angel's stare. When it didn't, she felt somewhat reassured, but went on exactly as if she weren't. "You could hurt her, Sam. What if she took you seriously?"

"It's in your imagination, Jen, so Socorro would have a hard time taking it seriously." He said "Socorro" lightly, without apprehension, without even a trace of the pleasure that having a reason to pronounce your lover's name—or even the name of someone you had once or twice imagined as your lover—to your wife might give, and Jenny, keenly alert to the possible inflections, was convinced, except for a last niggling doubt that turned erotic as soon as he left the bed. She drew the quilts to her side and anchored them slyly with knee and elbow. She heard the kindling rattling down, then the match, then the rustle of tinder catching, and again, after an interval in which Sam blew softly into the stove, sweet-talking it, the shudder of coals dropping, each thump softened by ash; then a hiss; then the closing moan of hinges, and he was back in bed, his feet cold, his hand moving along her leg. Wherever he stroked, there was a faint glitter of sensation she guessed was coal dust.

Late that afternoon, Jenny, coming into the kitchen to sweep the floor, found that the roof had leaked all along the butcher-block counter. She went into the yard, where Sam was cutting kindling, and asked him if he would sweep the snow from the flat roof. He drove the ax blade into a chunk of cedar, lifted ax and cedar together, and brought them down, splinters raining across Jenny's wet boots. "The roof," she said. "Please?"

"When I'm done."

She stalked away. He watched snow fall onto her dark hair and, though at that moment he disliked her, he began to whistle.

And was still whistling, on the roof, when he spotted the smallest of Socorro's boys sidling on his bottom along the fence rail, scooting along parallel to the bored progress of the sorrel horse, which seemed to be watching him from the corner of its eye. The little boy leaned from the fence into the horse's shoulder, catching its mane. Sam, who had been scooping the gutter clear with his gloved hands, let the ice fall. The horse began to canter, and at first, oddly, it cantered quite gently through the snow, dragging the boy, who was trying to get a leg over its back. Sam had an instant of hope. Ice rained from the roof's edge past the kitchen window where Jenny was day-dreaming; then she heard Sam's boots ringing down the ladder's rungs, and the metal flex of the ladder as he caught himself. He ran by the window. She went to the door, past the neat stack of new kindling, and began to run, plunging her left foot into his left boot print, her right into his right, as if she'd been told to take ten giant steps, fifty, a hundred, the snow's crust already broken by his knees but still biting into hers. The cold printed itself in her lungs. It illumined them—an X-ray she inhaled. There had never been such cold.

The boy had fallen flat on his back, one arm extended. Jenny had time to notice a line of rabbit tracks that disappeared under that arm and reappeared on the other side of his body. Sam stripped off his gloves. He tugged on the boy's jaw and felt inside for the tongue. Jenny saw baby teeth. He listened, then pinched the pale nose, crouched, and exhaled into the child's mouth. Jenny saw him guess at the duration, curbing his own intensity to keep it a child's breath, yet with every muscle in his body willing it to suffice. He lifted his face and panted, for he was still trying to catch his own breath, staring at her through the plumed air; he crouched, and she could see the infinite delicacy he brought to this breath, and the stillness in which he listened for its answer. Again he stared at her. His stares, each a fraction of a second, marked off the failed breaths. In another instant they would stare at each other over a dead child. She knew this in her knees, her mouth, her eyes, her throat, her bowels; she knew what it was going to be like; it would own them in a moment. She was so far ahead of herself that when

Sam lifted his face and a breath curled thinly along his cheek, she couldn't tell where it had come from. He was waiting for it to happen again. This time, when it did, at exactly the same moment Jenny and Sam said, "Ah."

It was as if they had said it to each other in sex. Jenny felt a great, rib-cage exultation. Sam slid a hand into the quilted, filthy snowsuit for the heartbeat. She knelt to talk to him.

"What happened?"

"He fell off the horse, and the horse stopped and kicked him. It just turned on him. A hoof caught him right in the chest. I can't find any blood, so I think we ought to get him into the house. Do you think it's all right to move him now?"

She stroked the boy's forehead. They were suddenly two adults with a child between them, and for some reason it felt familiar to her. "I think he'll freeze out here if you don't."

"Hey," Sam said. "Hey, *hito*, I know everything hurts, but does anything hurt especially much?" The boy shook his head; he coughed, then hiccuped, still shaking his head. "It's O.K.," Sam said. "Don't get too scared. You feel bad, but I don't think anything's broken. So you're going to stay kind of quiet and not talk. I want you to be my buddy now, all right? Remember who I am? I'm going to carry you home."

The horse had caught sight of Jenny. He lowered his head and his ears pitched forward; he took two hesitant steps toward them. On his chest there was a small patch of shadow. Jenny was impressed by this. How frightened he must be, to sweat so wildly in such cold. He swung his head around to be sure of her, and took another step. She admired once more the beauty in the shape of the dark eye, the vein that spindled from the saucer of cheek to the dilated nostril, and the pale forelock that stuck up between his pricked, attentive ears. Looking over Sam's shoulder, the boy hiccuped harder. Jenny stood. She shouted, stamping her feet and swinging her arms, and the horse ran.

{ Jenny knocked. When her knuckles made no sound, she took
her glove off and tried again. "Socorro?"

Socorro opened the door, holding one of her husband's shirts
on a hanger; she handed it to Jenny with a strangely sub-
missive gesture, as if that were what Jenny had come for, and
all she wanted. Then Socorro closed her eyes and leaned her
cheek into the doorjamb.

"Socorro, come on, he's all right," Sam said.

"It's me," Socorro said. "It's because of *me*."

"That's not true," Sam said.

"He's all right," Jenny said. "It's nothing bad. He's not
hurt."

"I don't think he even has any broken bones," Sam said.
"So can we come in?"

"He's all right?" Socorro put her hand to the boy's face; he
took a deep, rasping, relieved breath and began to cry. Sam,
rocking him lightly, carried him to the sofa, covered him with
a shawl, and each time a tear ran down his cheek swiped at it
with his forefinger and pretended to taste it.

"This one's not salty enough," Sam said.

"My husband isn't home to see this," Socorro said.

"Do you want me to call him for you?" Jenny was watching Sam with the boy.

"No, it's better if he comes home like always and finds out
then."

"It's better, you're sure?" Jenny was thinking, But what if
he doesn't come home at all, the way he sometimes doesn't?
Then she chided herself. It was purely Socorro's business. It was
none of her own.

"I think so," Socorro said. "I'm pretty sure. Tell me where
he was, Jenny? Tell me what happened?"

"This one is too salty," Sam said. "Now this one, thank God, this one is juuuuust right."

⟨ Juan did come home, at dusk, when a little more snow was falling. Jenny had gone out to get some kindling—she wanted to read in her chair with her feet tucked up, and that required a fire. Sam was in the yard, and looked up when she came out. They were standing like that, facing each other, when they heard the shot. The report ended bluntly, its echo skipping from facet to facet of the bluff behind them, so neither Jenny nor Sam was really sure what they had heard. It wasn't very different from the first stroke of an ax in cold air. Sam went to the rise where he could look down into the Gallardo field, and Jenny followed. There was Juan, still in his work clothes, hold-ing his pistol, and there was the horse, his head still lifted but turned away from Juan, then growing slowly heavy and sink-ing at an angle such that a cheek would strike the ground, not the nose; the tail flared, the hocks crippled under, and the long belly fell, thrusting rather lightly forward, the chest cracking the glaze of snow before it. The head lifted from the snow as Juan shot it again.

"Jesus Christ," Sam said.

For some reason, he put his hand over Jenny's mouth. He drew her back against himself.

The horse's neck was a bow—not the direction a horse's neck arches in, but its reverse. The torque of his neck was illustrated by his coarse mane. There was a great deal of blood; Juan was walking in it.

"Go in now, you bastard," Sam said softly.

Juan nudged the horse's nose with the toe of his boot, then walked to a place in his yard where the snow was still clean, stepped neatly in and out of a drift, and went into the house. Jenny, in Sam's arms, watched until smoke rose from the chimney, a thin strand that floated only a little way before unraveling.

"Jenny?" Sam said. "Tell me something. Just say you won't leave now—just that one small thing."

For what seemed like a long while they stood staring down at the house, but its door was closed for good.

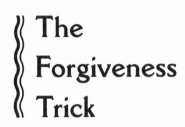

The Forgiveness Trick

In London, Nicholas, who was nearly five and had never been afraid of the dark before, began to need his father at night. Barefoot on the pricklish Oriental rug, Nicholas would feel his way through the sitting room, which was dark except for six high, fogged-over windows that smelled of cold rainy glass and dirty painted mullions—he knew because he liked to lean his forehead against them in the afternoon. At night, a sudden dappling of lights on the ceiling meant a taxi in the street below, passing the hotel where black cabs often idled; his mother liked to catch them there. These lights wavered, flared very white, then flying-saucered around the walls, taking the corners fast, dipping when they hit the plush back of an aged armchair. The taxi's sound was a sticky unreeling like a long, long strand of tape being pulled free from something; there were deep puddles the tires had gone through. Then it was quiet. London was quiet.

The thing that worried him most was when the cat came into the room. The cat belonged to two old English people who had gone away, leaving it, and their flat, in the care of the

Americans—Nicholas and his mother and father. The cat knew when Nicholas was awake: at the rug's far side it would fold itself into a crouch, steer its ears forward, and turn its sharpened attention, its small vexed mouth and round eyes, entirely on the child. Neither moved; this was hatred. Nicholas taunted it softly, "Fleas, fleas, fleas." The cat shied around antique-chair legs and was gone, leaving Nicholas alone.

At the door of his parents' room, he bumped his back rhythmically against the doorjamb in relief. The old radiator on the wall croaked and fluted as its metal pipes contracted; it was warmer in there than it had been downstairs, and he could see his mother's head behind his father's shoulder, and hear their different breathing. Going in, he stood by the bed until his father opened his eyes.

Nicholas's face, when touched in the dark by his father, had that charged, freshened feel it had after tears. All Charlie was aware of in that moment of sleepy chaos was fear, a wrench of hard alertness, which lasted until, his slightly more sensible self dawning, he realized that this had happened before, that this was only a night like the others when Nicholas had waked him because of a dream; it wasn't the surreal, sudden wrong Charlie believed could invade his life—his son hurt. If Charlie had felt what he felt on waking and not had Nicholas right before him, he would have gone crazy. He would have had to run until he found Nicholas, if it meant running ten miles. So he was grateful that there was just enough distance between them for his arm to stretch comfortably across. He loved the fit of his son's cheek in his hand. He caught some of the fine hair, tugged his son's head sideways, and said, "You and me, buddy."

Charlie conducted his son to the little bathroom, clicked the light on, and Kyra in the bed heard her husband whisper, "Niagara Falls," and then the patter of Nicholas's pee, followed by silence as they went back through the flat, then down the stairs, to Nicholas's room.

And Kyra, for whom sleep had vanished, didn't know what to do. She imagined herself sitting on the edge of a bed, sheltering Nicholas, rocking and murmuring through the first caught breaths and the hard hiccups, stroking the hair back from his hot forehead, wiping his nose, then cleverly eliciting the details of the dream, but that couldn't happen now that Nicholas wanted his *father*. In an excess of loneliness for them, she lay heeding the cranky radiator's groans (this place cost too much, and the nagging letters from its distant owners irritated her immensely. All those questions about their darling cat, when they had regarded Nicholas with the fastidious suspicion of the elderly and childless, and almost not rented the place to Charlie and Kyra, giving in at the last possible—). When Charlie wanted something, he started right in: London was this, London was that; the year's apprenticeship to an English publisher meant recognition of his worth. Then he went for her weaknesses: "New York is getting scarier, Ky. When Jay and Linda lived on Hampstead Heath, they let their three-year-old wander anywhere, and he says they felt perfectly safe. How long since we felt perfectly safe? He says London's sane. Think what it will mean to Nicholas to have one year of childhood when we're not watching him every sec." How could she have known to say no? She'd have felt selfish, one of the things she least liked feeling.

She cast her leg across Charlie's side. His absence was nice. Now she could think. There was so little thinking in families, such a ruckus of needy feeling. It seemed to her that Nicholas's dreams had to be her fault, that there was something she was capable of—some insight, some decision—and the dreams would be fanned away. She pushed her foot down to the cold bottom of the bed and found the cat there; he worked up a small, protesting yawn. She scooped him off the bed—a silken-slack sack, unresisting, that met the cold floor with a thump. The responsibility for Nicholas's nightmares was making her resentful, and she wanted to know what Charlie was doing. Going down the stairs she heard his voice. She didn't listen closely, but guessed from his intonation he wasn't getting anywhere.

In Nicholas's doorway, she got an update: "Something was in here," Charlie explained from the edge of the bed.

Kyra pushed her hair from her face. All she could think of to say was "What?" so she said, "What?" guiltily, to her husband and her small son.

"Tell me what," Charlie urged. Nicholas shook his head. He could go stubborn like that, on her, on his sitter, or on anyone. During the week, Charlie sealed himself away in that gray suite of Bedford Square offices; his lunches lasted all afternoon, his afternoons lasted until long after dark. Most of his precious year was up, and he tended to come home so exhausted that he hadn't yet picked up on something that should have been obvious: his son's head-shaking resistance was part of a phase, and basically had nothing to do with him. If he didn't watch out, Charlie was going to turn into the sort of father who pretended closeness but who really relied on briefings from his wife about their son's emotions. Kyra hated fathers like that.

Charlie insisted. "Can you start with what it looked like?"

Nicholas made a soft hissing, tongue to his front teeth: a child's embarrassment at being asked a question so far off the mark, so devoid of any intuition about the child's situation, that he is forced—briefly but with urgency—to wonder at the poverty of comprehension, which seems to imply that he is not at the heart of his father's world. Nicholas would have forgotten it completely in a minute, Kyra knew, but she didn't like that he had had to feel it. She imagined that her eyes were firing tiny red darts into Charlie's big, dense back.

He didn't turn. He said, "Nicky, you got me out of bed because of it. Don't you think I deserve to know something about it?"

Blackmail, Kyra thought. Wrong wrong wrong. Blackmail was the last thing that worked with Nicholas.

Her son's head shook fiercely, No, no, no. He fitted his shoulders more closely against the wall, put his chin on his kneecap, and gripped his ankles painfully hard. What he wanted to do now, Kyra was sure, was to distract his father from this course of questioning. He was trying to make his feet turn white. He gazed intently at his toes, waiting for the blood to be cut off.

"He doesn't want to talk about it yet," Kyra offered from the doorway.

"Ky, that's good. That's great. Undo what I've done. We were getting somewhere."

"You were not; look at him."

"I needed two more minutes; that's just like you."

"Stop it, then." She thought, *Pig.* She was amazed to have thought that about Charlie. *Pig?*

"What are you smiling about?" he demanded. "Have you got a lover?"—a question so astonishing, so out of the blue, that Charlie froze where he was, looking over his shoulder at her, and she froze where she was, neither of them immediately believing, but both then hearing, far too clearly, the unforgiving automatic inner replay of his words. She knew it was one of those things that just slip out; she knew that Charlie would never forget that it had slipped out in front of Nicholas; she knew that Charlie was going to worry the possible future psychological complexities of that for a long time. Thus far, they'd been so cunning in keeping their problems to themselves, even the affair Charlie had strayed into and out of in New York last March. They'd wished into place over Nicholas a rainbowed security, and neither had ever before let the tremors between them trouble it. She did a quick mother's scan: Nicholas didn't look as if he'd heard a thing. "Lover"—what could that conceivably mean to four-and-a-half? Nothing. He was staring, with satisfaction, at his toes. More than anything, Kyra wished to pry his fingers from his feet.

To Nicholas, Charlie said in a stricken tone, "You won't talk to me."

His voice was hoarse. It was too much emotion to address a child with; it could only confuse Nicholas more. In a protective rush, Kyra said, "Hey, no more tonight, guys."

Charlie slid from the bed and knelt. He covered his face and said through his fingers, "Why won't you?" Frightened, Kyra thought: He's going to cry. But he only said, "What am I doing that changed you?" He couldn't see the startled glance his son gave him.

Kyra could. "Up, Charlie," she said. "Back to bed now. Come on, old bear."

Nicholas said to her over his father's head, "No, *you* go." When she didn't move, he bounced against the wall in irritation and shouted, "You go! You go!"

"Nicholas," she pleaded, "I—"

"Nicholas Chinaman Cincinnati," Charlie said, lifting his head, the purifying light of nonsense in his eye. "In the morning, see, you and I are going to get down to business. I love you, and that's it. That's all you need to know before you start talking to me, because I get this feeling more and more lately like something's wrong, and I'm your father, and I'm going to make it stop being wrong, see, because that's my job." Charlie kissed his son's forehead, though Nicholas, still scrunched up against the wall, tried to duck to the side. "God, he still smells great," Charlie said to Kyra. "Let's do it again. Let's have a baby in grotty old, gray old London. His hair's wonderful. I can't believe it. I love every cell of you," he said to Nicholas. "I love every atom in your body and the spaces between atoms—don't be frightened, they're just little spaces—and I love your fingernails, even bitten down to nothing, and the backs of your hands that're so chapped, and the insides of your ears, and your ear-drums, and I love your brain, and your teeth, and the way your tongue looks—stick it out, ah, that's ugly, that's pathetic. I love your elbows and your knees and your navel. Did I leave anything out?"

"My penis," Nicholas said. He was giggling wildly. "My *penis.*"

"Nothing wrong with you," Charlie said. "That's the life force speaking up. When you were inside your mom—listen to this—the doctor said you had the strongest heartbeat she'd heard in twelve years of listening to babies."

"Me?" Nicholas said. "In Mom? I was the strongest?"

"Out of a lot of babies listened to, yes, you were. You really were. Now, are you O.K. to be left?"

He was; suddenly he was. Charlie climbed the stairs behind Kyra, and his hands framed her bottom as it ascended, bracketed it lightly on either side, though he didn't touch her. "What do you think the dream was?" he asked, when they were in their own bed. The room seemed to have gotten much colder in their absence. She shook her head softly in the dark, knowing he could feel the movement, and then said, "What do you think?"

"Whatever it was, if he was scared, why would he want you to go away?"

"I don't know that either." Then she remembered. "Charlie, why did you ask me if I had a lover?"

"Christ, in front of him."

"I know. So why?"

"I know you don't have a lover."

"Then why did you open your mouth and have that come out?"

"Crazy."

"I wanted to kill you," she said.

"You should have. London was never what you wanted, right? So it's been strange, us being in England because of me, with nothing here for you. It could have come between us."

"It could have."

"In the office lately, I wonder, 'What is she doing right now?' In New York, I don't know, I was beginning to feel remote from you. Now it's back the way it used to be."

"Why? Why now, Charlie?"

"Dunno, sweet. Do not know."

"Sweet" was an old endearment, possibly their first. It meant that Charlie was a senior at the University of Michigan, she a green-eyed girl who'd glanced up from a coffee cup to find, directed her way across the jammed cafeteria, a scrutiny she'd rather theatrically returned. Now she was grateful no such look was possible. He could find things out only through her voice. She kept it calm. "But why not have loved me like that in New York? Why now?"

"That's what I ask myself. And I don't know, so I haven't brought it up before. I just want us to get through these last months and be back in New York still us. I meant I need you."

In the dark her mouth went round, considering, then indented at the corners in a smile, because she had felt that swift internal tug, deep as instinct, by which she knew the truth when any of three people told it: Charlie, or Nicholas, or—not least useful—herself. She was still smiling when he rolled over and caught the point of her chin between his teeth. They were breathing each other's breath. "Away," she said. "I have to yawn." He let go, and she yawned. She still felt a dazzling white spot of hatred for him, which she wouldn't have been conscious of if he hadn't insisted on being so close to her—but the thing he had done was a huge thing.

He rested his cheek against her shoulder, she rested her chin against his head and, flicking his dark hair very lightly with her fingertips, she said, "Sleep," and pushed him away.

She had an irritated sense of their straining to be silent together, each aware of how the least movement might, this far into the night, prove unbearable to the other, and of how stranded they were, really, with sleep receding farther and farther from probability. Yet she must have been napping, because she was snatched awake when she heard, "I can't sleep."

"You feel so bad."

"Yes."

Her dislike was so great she couldn't fashion a question for him. She simply said, "About."

"Christ, in front of him. I mean you and I, we can understand, we're equipped—"

"He's all right," she said. "He's a child. They have—they have some kind of protection. I mean we all had childhoods, and we turned out all right. Look at us."

"Comforting," he said.

She was exhausted. "It is and isn't," she said.

But she was awake enough to pity Charlie, feeling for him the insinuation of guilt into his future, guilt toward his son, and her heart did its forgiveness trick. Often after the very worst moments in their marriage, she had experienced a blithe instant in which she was all lightness, all reckless tenderness toward Charlie, as if nothing he did was beyond her power to understand and endure, yet as if those things were suddenly immensely easy to forgive, far easier than it could ever have looked from outside —but there was nobody outside, of course. It was a marriage. There had been somebody outside, but there wouldn't be, after tomorrow.

}} Hannah's Example

W hen Caro is really furious at Hart, she consoles herself with thinking what his heart is the size of: his heart is the size of a *pea*; his heart is the size of a *pin*head; his heart— she gazes with hot malice at her own little fingernail—is no bigger than *that*. But mostly it is the image of the pea—dry, rattly-hard, withered up completely—that sustains her.

Lying late in the rumpled bed, Caro crosses her long-johnned legs, draws her knees to her chest, and grasps her ankles in a stretch meant to lengthen the muscles of her thighs. Though she's two months pregnant, and various alien emotions have been washing through her, it's not like her to be so absorbed in this particular daydreaming spite. This is a mood that might have been borrowed intact from Hart's ex-wife, Hannah.

If, in her silently blazing WASP way, Hannah had been almost continually angry at Hart, she'd almost continually had reason. Hart's infidelities tended to be spur-of-the-moment, thoughtless things, but they were frequent, too frequent for his wife's increasingly embittered resistance. Hannah's example has caused Caro to swear two things to herself, as safeguards for her future. First, she will never try to stick with Hart through his being unfaithful to her, because she knows how that ended for Hannah: each tenterhooks reconciliation was ruined by yet another, though better concealed, phase of cheating. Caro had been Hart's final, serious betrayal of his fair-haired wife, because Caro's energy proved more than Hannah could withstand. The purity of Caro's determination to have her husband had undercut Hannah's nerve so completely that she'd lost her resilient old hope of winning Hart back, rendering him faithful, and piecing her family together again. Maybe this was finally revealed to Hannah for what it was, an impossibility. When the fight went out of Hannah, her looks—which had always made Caro feel so small and Third World, such an unlikely intruder into Hannah's existence—went too. In that cruel time, Caro had once had to wait in the car while Hart called at the door of his ex-house for his son. It was a lesson that Caro, her chin on the steering wheel, had absorbed, first absently and then with rising disbelief: tall, threatening Hannah was gone, and in the doorway, wearing a soiled, safety-pinned kimono, stood another, supplanted Hannah, a smudge of jam over her left breast, her dirty braid slipping over her shoulder as she dumped her mewing cat to the ground and caught Kevin by the elbows to kiss him good-bye.

Kevin had fine posture from his dance classes and displayed a nervy courtesy under his mother's long caress, though his father and his father's new girl friend were watching. Hannah's glare grew fixed almost to craziness when she aimed it at the car where Caro waited, Caro who at that moment abandoned all fear of Hannah except the fear that, in seeming so completely undone, she would at last seduce Hart back to old responsibilities—responsibilities he'd never disliked, after all, but only been unable to meet. From a huge, intricately competitive family of Nicaraguan exiles, Caro understood very well the seductive undertow of true need, when you find it directed at you. It was possible that desperate Hannah would find a way to make it work for her.

That hadn't happened; in fact, its opposite had, for the needier Hannah appeared—and for a time she seemed quite precarious—the more decisively estranged from her Hart became. Thus, Caro's second Hannah-lesson learned, and her second law laid down for herself. She will never let herself fall apart the way Hannah had, not where Hart can see. She will never so visibly suffer.

Now that she and Hannah are on wary good terms, and it is the two of them who negotiate which weeks Kevin will spend with his father and which with his mother, Caro often regrets what the older woman went through, but thinking back to that time she discovers nothing she can really imagine changing, nothing she would alter even now, and no way that she, the more willful, does not end up married to Hannah's husband.

Even now, now that the kind of attention she's needed from Hart is light-years beyond what she's been getting. She's been so thoroughly cheated of it that tears come to her eyes when she remembers that affection for a pregnant wife is not only possible, but natural and right, its absence a sign that something has gone very wrong. It would be easier to forget what is her due, face the way things are with Hart, and try to make the best of them. But she is a daughter of the Dominguez clan, now spread triumphantly across North America, with her younger brother ensconced with his WATS line in Washington, finding American slots for other refugees, and their widowed mother seated straight-backed behind the old black Singer in the austere light of a Brooklyn window, her winged fingers gliding the cloth under the quick needle as they have done since Caro's earliest memory. And when any of the Dominguezes had been trying to make the best of something, there had been all of those other Dominguezes around, chortling over the twist of fate by which an enemy's hopes were ruined, cooing over a new romance, cursing setbacks in business. And then so expertly, deftly (as only Dominguezes knew how) teasing you into a stronger frame of mind, so that it was never as if you were alone in what happened to you. It was as if you had a number of other, stauncher selves to fall back on when you yourself finally felt defeated.

The gathered Dominguezes, their heads uniformly dark as blackbird wings, chortled at the wedding, too. They were Dominguezes, and they'd always nurse a deep skepticism about someone who wasn't a Dominguez, but Hart was clearly in love with her then, so the Dominguezes kissed Caro and then stood on their tiptoes, even the hard-of-hearing old aunts in their glorious hats, to kiss this foreigner they were trusting with their beloved Caro. Lately Caro steals the phone bill from the mail before Hart can find it, and though he's never asked for it, she's afraid eventually he will—afraid he's going to discover how wild she is for Dominguez voices and that keen, blackbird-eyed point of view on her present mess.

Caro eases her leg down Hart's side of the bed, finding nothing but cold sheets. She lets her toenails rasp, running her foot under the linen—a sound Hart can't stand, but this is a trick she's practiced since she was small, and used it to drive her spoiled prince of a younger brother mad. She didn't have many weapons against him, and he could be mean, coiling a dead jade-green grass snake around the outhouse seat. Why is it so radiantly comforting to find, now that she's twenty-nine and married and pregnant, that she still has this resource against her little brother, who is twenty-eight and far away, sealed into his soundproofed D.C. cubicle with only good intentions in his heart?

She listens, trying to place her husband, and can't, though she doesn't feel quite left yet, either. Her sense of what the house is like when it's empty except for her is by now so refined it's unerring. He must have got up in the night to pace out some problem in his precious mathematics, prowling the living room or dreaming out the window at the moonlit, faintly flashing river, which fascinates him almost as much as imaginary numbers, and which was his chief reason for coveting this old house, before they bought it. Caro envies him, sometimes: the river is such an unfailing enchantment for him. She was reckless to pretend, when he fell in love with this isolated house in the gorge, that she felt something like that enchantment, that she wouldn't mind being alone, or count the husbandless hours. Having believed her, Hart can only feel deceived when they argue over just those issues—the house's remoteness, her alone-ness—but the truth is that she'd banked on her power to divert him from his schedule of commuting fifty miles each way, three days a week, to teach. The house is fine with him in it, and she'd unwisely assumed he'd find it less and less easy to be away so much, and finally revise his situation in the clarifying light of heartache. Instead, he'd maneuvered to keep things as they were: when his chairman had inquired whether Hart would like to spend more time at home this semester, Hart hadn't relinquished a single teaching hour. *Because* she's pregnant, he'd argued, they can't let their income be whittled away; he knows what a child costs, even if she has, as yet, no idea. There are nights when, exhausted, he blanks out on his office couch and can't rouse himself to brave the cold wind in the deserted parking lot and the drive that follows, nights when, needing him, having confessed to needing him, she is more bitterly alone than ever.

Caro rasps her toenails one last resentful scrape down the sheet, and rolls over, feeling the light now fully focused on her face, to find a black widow policing the windowpane above her head. The spider is large and moves as if contact with the brilliant, backlit glass is painful to it; it does not so much set its legs on the glass as needle them at it, and the black droplet of its abdomen has a cumbersome, clinging weight, cradled within the agitation of its dainty legs. Caro sits up, driving herself with a thrust of her feet to the bed's far edge, and screams for Hart. It is as if a shock of sound stuns the spider: it freezes, and then, at a ticking run, it reaches the sill and strikes a fly that is caught in frowsy strands of web.

Caro knows Hart is in the doorway because an animal relief fans through her before he says a word. She turns, and forgives him everything, he is so solid, so tall, and so stricken with fear for her.

"Christ, Caro, what?"

She points, rocking in her impatience for him to act. The spider is ticking up the glass again, very fast, bearing its swaddled fly. "Hart, kill it before it gets away."

"What for?" he says.

"It's a black widow." She is amazed at having to explain; his solid bigness changes, at that moment, from comforting to almost stupid.

"You're sure?"

Now his barefooted stance, she sees, is that of reluctance, but why? "Get it, or it's going to hide itself, and then there will be others."

Coming closer, squinting judiciously, he says, "Black widows are very elusive. They hate human beings."

"They hate them. They *kill* them."

"It's not acting elusive, so how do you know it is one?"

"It wanted that fly. It got that fly. It will act elusive again in a second. Now will you kill it?" Springing from bed, she finds only her red Reeboks. She doesn't want them soiled with spider; she kneels and draws a loafer of Hart's from farther under the bed. She holds it out, dancing on her long-johnned legs in her need for him to do what she wishes. He laughs at her, and she strikes his chest with the shoe. He doesn't catch it; it falls to the floor. He is going to defeat her.

"You're *afraid*," she says. From his face, she knows she has caught on; and understanding him when he intends to be opaque seems such an incredible stroke of luck that, even in her fury, she is steadied by it, calmed enough to try again. "Hart, that's poison carried by that spider, and it can hurt one of us, and if you don't care about us, *me*, then care about the baby crawling and—"

"I told you, black widows are very elusive."

Kevin has come into the room and is watching them with detached wonder, as if nothing they do can really surprise him.

"That one will come back!" she screams, pointing.

"All right," he says, tremendously cold. "You insist that I kill it."

She hands him his shoe, but what she feels is curious: it is pity. He takes two staggering, kneeling steps on the bed, the mattress jolting under his weight, and his first swat misses. His second goes wide as well, sending the spider racing diagonally down the window. Hart hits it, but weakly. The shoe lifts away; the spider starts out in crippled imitation of its former perfect self, and Kevin and Caro cry out together. The spider has almost made it to a chink in the sill when Hart, flinching, finishes it off with a series of hammering blows.

Caro reads his back: he is absolutely furious.

"Hey," Kevin says. "That was wild, you two guys yelling." Earringed, with the shy grit of a new beard along his jaw, he is wearing an enormous fisherman's sweater and a pair of pin-striped pajama bottoms. Nearly as tall as his father, he runs a hand through his hair, which stands up in a prison-camp burr. When Caro first met him, that hair was limp as a baby's and fell into his eyes. She thought he'd be her enemy, but she'd been wrong.

"Caro was yelling," Hart says. "It scared her."

Husband and wife trade a clear, cold stare.

"It didn't scare you, did it, Hart? Tell Kev how you kept your head. How you almost let it get away. But he saw that part."

"There are black widows in the woodpile behind Mom's house," Kevin says. Sometimes he calls his mother "Mom," sometimes "Hannah." "She says now that the weather's changing, they're trying to get inside. She warns me about them all the time. She's kind of intense about it."

So not only Kevin but, subtly, Hannah is an ally of hers. Caro's anger lightens, and she feels a little better, though she's tired and her stomach wobbles, as it does so often in the mornings. One sign from Hart, and the quarrel can end. She searches his expression, and very gradually, so that it won't be too obvious, he relents: after all, he is facing his young wife and his anxious son. He says, "I killed it. So O.K., everyone?"

"O.K. with me," Kevin says. "I forgot, Hannah called. She wanted to know if she can borrow your chain saw Saturday."

"Tell her no."

"I told her yes. She has a permit to cut piñon in the canyon up behind her house, and they hardly ever give permits for there anymore."

Hart sighed. "We can all go Saturday, then, and split a pickup load. We need wood here, too."

"Great," Kevin says, a little too exuberantly, and adds, in the interest of peace, "She'll like that."

Peace is difficult for Caro—her adrenaline is running too high—but obedient to the father-and-son camaraderie a newly formed plan always seems to call forth, she goes softly down the stairs and cracks eggs for their omelet.

⦃ The three o'clock sun cuts in a wintry way among the cold
⦃ black columns of ponderosa and lights the fallen needles that
form tortoiseshell drifts against downed trees. Few of these are

good for firewood. Hart and Kevin pass them by, the chain saw slanting heavily from Kevin's gloved hand: the fallen piñon is punky and smells damply, earthily, of its decay. Sometimes stopping to consider a tree, shaking their like heads, father and son climb the ridge until they are out of sight. Finally, from the ridge's far side, the chain saw pierces the settled silence of the woods. A grinding series of false starts, an echoing wait, and then the hot, rising roar as the engine catches.

Hannah had left the house where she was Hart's wife, and found, in the country, the ruin of a many-roomed, once beautiful adobe. It seemed a strange move for Hannah, fragile as she was following the divorce, and maybe a further slide away from the real world, but the house steadied her and left her resourceful, and with a new mood: the neutral reasonableness, toward men, of women who live alone. She and a boyfriend began wiring the house for electricity, and when the boyfriend disappeared, she fished out his repair manual and finished the job herself, then sanded the kitchen floor down to its natural pine pallor, which had been hidden beneath decades of grime. She unstopped the chimneys of birds' nests, dealt with field mice, and carted the attic's assortment of detritus to the dump. Because the house is still heated only by wood stoves, and piñon is going for sixty-five dollars a cord, she needs this wood run. She and Caro are shagging kindling into the pickup's bed, and Caro admires the strength in Hannah's arms. Since she's been pregnant, Caro's own breathing feels shallow, and goes raspy after even mild exertion.

Hannah pauses and leans against the pickup, wiping her forehead with the cuff of her sawdusty glove. This leaves a smudge, and Caro thinks of the jam on the ragged, long-ago kimono. Caro leans beside her, at first gingerly and then at full slouch, and Hannah says, "Duck your head." When Caro does, Hannah unfastens wood chips like barrettes from Caro's curls, and a gratefulness almost erotic in its intensity sweeps through

Caro, lulling her. "Your hair's so great," Hannah says. "So wild. You've no idea how I hated you for having it. It meant you had more energy than me."

I knew, Caro thinks, but says, "Yours is exactly the kind of hair we wanted, all my sisters and me, when we were little. Princess hair. It was what we saw in movies."

"No, it's mouse hair. Dull, Anglo hair." Hannah tastes a cedar sliver, and tosses it away. "Hart's going to have some strategy for loading the pickup that we've just violated."

"Heaviest wood on the bottom, or something. But we couldn't stand around waiting. And I don't feel like climbing that ridge and helping drag wood down. They could've found something closer."

Hannah studies her with interest. "You know, it's nice for Kevin to get a day like this with Hart. Times like this, when they're just being macho together with a chain saw, have been rare."

"I know."

"You can't know," Hannah says, with a slight, cutting trace of her old resentment. "You haven't been keeping track, and I have. I can't help it. I have. I suppose I should feel jealous for Kevin now that you're pregnant, because this baby will take even more of his father's time away from him, but if Kev can't feel that, it seems—oh, almost vicious—to feel it for him." She slouches prettily against the pickup, looking far less angry than she sounds, looking, in fact, almost musingly peaceful. "Kevin likes the idea of this baby."

What do you think about it, Caro wonders. "He'll be a good big brother," she says.

"You know, I think you should try something with Hart that I never tried."

Caro is startled. "What's that?"

"Whoever Hart was, even if he was, say, stronger than he is, it wouldn't be easy for him to handle not only Kevin but a brand-new child. He's caught between what fathers feel for nearly grown sons and what entirely new fathers feel, and those emotions are nothing alike." Hannah twirls a twig as if it is the most fascinating thing she's seen that day. "Those opposite pulls can't be easy for Hart to reconcile, even for the sake of a very wanted baby."

It is half a question, and Caro doesn't answer, for fear the truth will acquire a falsely defiant ring in the telling: Of course Hart badly wants this baby.

"So what I'm recommending to you is something I was incapable of: that you trust him."

Again, Caro's startled. "But you, you were incredibly trusting with him."

Hannah laughs. "Is that how it looked? I was in love. I went to great lengths. I forgave a lot, but I suspected a lot. I had this feeling that whatever I did, he'd always be one jump ahead of me, and I thought I had to fight that. Now I see that's the wrong way to act with him, because he's not ahead, he's behind. He's reacting. You have to go along as if you know, in the end, that you can count on him, because Hart has a way of living up to expectations."

She would have gone on—Caro yearns for her to go on— but Kevin is returning down the ridge, dragging a piñon trunk that sleds roughly over the fallen needles. His ax is driven deep into the wood, and he leans forward, pulling against the tree's weight with measured, adult strides. Hannah regards him with pleasure when he comes up to her, panting, and lets the ax fall. "Look, Hannah." He embraces a ponderosa and rests his nose against its shaggy bark. "Do this."

"Why?"

"Just do."

Hannah chooses another, taller ponderosa, wraps her arms around it, and rests the tip of her nose against it.

"Now breathe deep."

"Vanilla," she says. "Vanilla, exactly. I never knew that."

"Hart showed me."

They stand, sniffing, their shoulders similarly set in delight. Hart appears, a trimmed section of piñon riding his shoulders like a yoke, to mock-frown at Kevin and Hannah. "I guess," he says, "that you're going to stand there an hour, right?"

"Oh, Hart," Hannah says. "What a secret." Mother and son move away from their trees together. Kevin tousles her hair with his dirty glove, and Hart slaps Kevin's back. After too long a moment they realize that Caro is leaning against the pickup.

It's dark by the time they've finished retrieving the cut wood from the steep ridge.

〈 In her kitchen, Hannah tamps tinder into the fuel box of the
〈 temperamental Garland, coaxing it to light, a heap of struck matches growing on the stove lid. "Hey," she finally says, gratified, letting the stove lid clank back into place. "This should get us warm in about twenty minutes, all right? You don't have a lot of choices for dinner. How about hamburgers? I think there's salsa."

"Anything," Hart says. "I'm starved."

Hannah's jeans tighten around her bottom as she peers into her refrigerator, shaking her head. "How about not hamburgers, but curry."

"Curry," Kevin says. "Caro's never had your curry."

"Will it be too hard for your stomach, Caro?"

Caro says no, though in fact she's not sure. She can't bear to seem like a bad sport when Hannah seems to have little enough to choose from. Hannah cooks with the nonchalant untidiness of a woman used to having her kitchen to herself, testing the sauce by licking her fingertip, stopping to feed and cajole the wood stove's fire. There are dirty dishes everywhere, and then a salad, pita bread, and chicken curry that burns Caro's tongue when she tries it. She wishes she could drink wine with the others. Jealously she watches the bottle pass among them, half-empty, empty. The well water from Hannah's tap tastes strange, like cold, iron-bearing stones.

"I like dinners like this." Hannah is sitting cross-legged on the bench drawn up to the scarred picnic table. "When everyone's too tired to talk, and just eats and eats. It's like a good old farm kitchen."

"You should know," Hart says. "You were a good old farm girl."

"Who went to Radcliffe," Kevin says.

"Who went, and learned next to nothing," Hannah says. "None of the important things. I learn more now."

"Like what do you learn?" Kevin scrubs his plate with pita for the last sauce.

"Like how I still need nerve." Hannah smiles, exercising a self-assured woman's prerogative: exposing a weakness to a man flirtatiously, knowing she'll lose nothing by it. "I found a black widow this morning, and it freaked me out. I couldn't kill it. I didn't realize until then that you'd been killing them for me, Kev, whenever I found one."

"Where was it?" Hart asks.

"Right above the coat hooks by the door," Hannah says, and Caro thinks, All she has to say to him is *Right above the coat hooks by the door* and he's on his feet.

"But it won't be there now," Hannah says.

"It's there," Hart says.

"I took all the coats down," Hannah says, "so that it wouldn't get into a pocket. I had this fear, all of a sudden, of Kevin sticking his hand into a pocket and there's the spider. Those things are like a bad dream." Hart lifts a broom and stirs a cobweb in a corner of the ceiling. The cobweb is sooty, and collects driftingly around the broomstick, like iron shavings to a magnet. The crabbed run of the spider is distinct as it darts out, angling down the wall. It has the evasive, hasty alertness of a little bird; it knows it is in danger, and this makes Caro shiver. There is a row of mucky boots, fallen gloves, and tattered sneakers on the floor. Hart lifts a sneaker, and when the spider is within arm's length, he snaps the shoe down. The *thock* is final. He says, "There," though he continues staring at the wall as if he's not convinced.

"I hate them," Hannah says. "I don't feel that way about anything else that gets into the house, but I hate, hate, hate black widows." She rests her shoulders against the wall, tips her head back, and settles into a kind of disturbed radiance, disturbed because the spider was there, radiant because it's been taken care of.

Hart, turning, finds Caro giving Hannah a look that could kill, though Hannah, her eyes closed, is unaware of it. Worse, Caro sees it dawn on Hart, slowly but inevitably: Hannah is beautiful.

So what can Caro do, where can she go? Home: her mother's fingers fly, stitching, arranging, bringing together the delicate pieces. A baby needs so many things.

⟩⟩ Migrants

Sissy isn't a small-town girl at heart—only through a steady refusal of circumstances, luck and love, to align themselves her way. Two years ago, Sissy's mother left Iowa with her boyfriend for L.A.; now they manage a trailer park of unpaved lanes and old palms whose lowest branches are dead, dry fans. Sissy's father sells the big Rain Cats, irrigation sprinklers that pivot around fields cut circular to accommodate them, the air above the pipes stunned with heat, the winter wheat below abruptly glistening, so that a long shadow seems towed by the sprinklers across a solid light-tan plane. Immediately below the pipes is the dividing line, drawn slowly forward, between drenched and parched, with the crossed wheat darkening in a sharp stretch and throwing off a thin, prismatic spume, or entire moving rainbows no bigger than birds' wings. Someday, Rafer says in his sales pitch, all of this will be run by computers, and in a far field the linked arms of Rain Cats will spring to life whether anyone is there to see them or not.

Just after Sissy's junior year of high school, Rain Cat

relocated Rafer to Wheaton, Colorado, and paid for the May-flower van. Sissy left a boyfriend Rafer didn't know about; Rafer left a bowling-alley waitress Sissy did. His new territory is vast and marginal, dusty fields of wheat, alfalfa, soybeans, and sugar beets worked by wetbacks and owned by farmers who are barely making it and already have too much capital tied up in obsolete heavy equipment—the kind of men, Rafer says, who shyly tap toothpicks from the plastic dispenser beside the cash register when they finally pay for the cup of coffee they nursed all morning long, and whose own fathers were so poor they cut the eyes from potatoes, planted the eyes, and boiled the potatoes to feed their families. All spring in Wheaton, where she knows no one and nobody seems to be under forty anyway, Sissy has been lonely; all spring Rafer has been on the road. Once when she thought she was cracking up, he warned her long-distance, "Sissy, it's a good thing I'm gone. If I wasn't gone, would I be making sales?" More gently, "Don't you know I go through this all week because I want a future for you?" Gentlest of all, "You're not going to grow up into one of those women who thinks the world owes them a living."

"Daddy, don't talk like that." Because she knew he meant her mother.

"We're in this together, aren't we? You just want to keep your head. I know that I can count on you."

Rafer says she shouldn't live for the weekends, but on Saturday nights they eat steak in a restaurant and he tells her about his week. Sunday mornings they take Joe, Rafer's dog, and his old .22, and drive out to one of the arroyos where a million shattered bottles lie, and Rafer steadies her arm while she shoots chips of glass, and sometimes dimes, from the eroded wall. She likes the way the dust floats up and smokes away. When they come home her hair is always lighter, her shoulders sunburned, and she cooks dinner for them both. Joe licks Rafer's face to wake him up, weekend mornings, and Rafer lifts Joe's floppy ear and sings into it as if it's a microphone, until Joe growls.

Sissy stops her bicycle at a windmill far out in the grasslands —stops as if windmill water, scummed with algae the dead landlocked green of pool-table felt, has some faint connection to clear Rain Cat water; stops as if Rafer, wherever he is, can feel her stopping. Though there seems to be no wind, the windmill blades keep turning, and blades of shadow switch with light on Sissy's face. The heat pausing on her cheek is pleasant, though she's almost sure the part in her hair is burning, her forehead and nose flecking with more ugly sharp freckles. Now that she's resting, the gloss of sweat, absent throughout the long bike ride, pricks her shaved armpits—a feeling like the beginning of a rash. A mourning dove lands on the holding tank's rim, peers at Sissy, fails to see her, and flutters to the ground, which is rutted by thousands of sunbaked cattle tracks, hoping to find a track that still cradles an inch of sour water. It used to puzzle her that the birds wouldn't bathe in the holding tank, but then she figured it out—it is impossible for a dove to drown in a cattle track.

She tips her bicycle up and walks it back to the highway, studying low bluffs that fade backward into a line of identically eroded, shades-paler bluffs; under the shadows of small moving clouds, the bluffs seem to be folding and unfolding. Between her and them lie a hundred miles that are nothing but empty. After that a thousand miles, and after that, L.A. Ah, she hates it here. *Hates* it. From dry weeds drawn into the bicycle spokes, a hail of grasshoppers patters against her bare legs. When their wings flick open, oval dapples form glaring eyes precise down to the honey iris and darker pupil. The eyes wink out as the grasshoppers fasten again onto trembling grass, and Sissy looks behind her at the bicycle's snaking track. All that way for what? For nothing.

But the highway radiates a tarry heat different from the heat of the grass, and exchanging one for the other is a relief. For an hour, by the watch loose on her sweating right wrist, she is the only moving thing in that landscape. Stranded on the horizon is a peaked farmhouse, gray with weather, its frame sides narrow as shutters closed against noon. This farmhouse has always depressed Sissy. She shakes her head, the bicycle wobbles dangerously, and from behind there is a blare of sound, rusty but convincing. Astonished, she looks over her shoulder to find a gypsy line of junk cars, moving probably at thirty miles an hour, so that, as they very gradually gain on her, she can drink it in: the candied sweetness of hot car paint, a whiff of burning engine oil and the cigarette smoke of the drivers, who are all young Spanish men; the charred doors wired shut with coat hangers, windshields that are cobwebs of fracture sealed by graffiti of yellowed tape; other windows ballooning with wet shirts or hung with ragtag, brilliant bits of underwear; grandmothers sleeping in the improvised shade of diapers flapping as they dry. Sissy loves them for having appeared behind her, out of nowhere. The dusty dashes hold groves of plastic saints, and rosaries wag from the rearview mirrors. A child sucking on its fist pushes aside a pair of fluttering pantyhose and gazes out at her. Another child pushes up beside the first, yawns widely, peels up a damp T-shirt, and shyly scratches a scarred chest. Sissy, too, feels shy. She is so exposed on the bicycle. They're migrants, she knows, up from Mexico for the summer. That too is cause for shyness, because the migrants who camp and work in the fields around Wheaton are shunned by the Anglos. Rafer has told her some cruel things he's seen.

The grown women all seem to be sleeping, many with children sprawled across their laps. Sleeping children look so much hotter than sleeping adults, Sissy thinks. They look as if they've fainted, their hands loose and their hair stuck to their foreheads. She laughs when a passing car shows the soles of two tiny bare feet resting flat against a window rolled halfway up. The heels are black. Gusts of real heat hit Sissy between the cars. She feels she belongs with them now, and resists falling behind. She chooses a Cadillac with scorched fins and burnt-out taillights, and tires herself in keeping alongside it; she wonders whether the driver, who never once glances sideways, has speeded up a little to lose her, and then she wonders at the enraged alarm she feels, knowing that he has. It is a brief battle. The Cadillac noses gently, very gently, into her lane, and she is forced to slow onto the shoulder. She feels flat amazement: Why did he do that? The Cadillac eases back into line, and the cars are gone. The highway's two lanes go desolate, the silence extremely definite. She sees a Coke bottle someone threw from a window. The bottle is rolling down the yellow line above its own delicately coasting shadow, to a hollow tone that seems to come from far away.

In Wheaton's post office there is a clerk, nearsighted Mr. Cox, who loves twiggy young trees fresh from the nursery, and Sissy likes him for that, though he is old and often cranky. Sprinklers fret across the dozen new dogwoods staked along the sidewalks, their slim trunks bandaged in gauze like the legs of colts. "Good for you, Coxy," Sissy says to herself. In fact, according to Rafer, Mr. Cox is less hostile to wetbacks than post-office clerks in the surrounding small towns are, and on Saturdays the migrants can be found, in from the fields, patiently waiting for Mr. Cox to hand them the money orders necessary to convey their entire paychecks home to Mexico. The ruined cars that passed Sissy three weeks ago in the grasslands are lined up now along the yellow curb in front of the post office. She glances into an ancient Chevrolet with a corroded hood; an empty baby bottle is nested upright in a child's torn sneaker. She shoulders open the glass door, and the men inside, scarcely turning, make way for her so subtly that she sees only their shaven napes, sunburned even through the darkness of the skin, and the backs of thin white shirts showing the ghosts of undershirts. There is a good, sharp barbershop smell. She stands, biting her lower lip, while the line dissolves away from her, the men gravitating toward a wall of wanted posters, making it seem that there is something irresistible and natural in their attraction to this wall.

Mr. Cox, squinting up from his scales, sees her standing alone. "Well, Sissy," he says. "This is a pleasure. Come on up."

"I can't, Mr. Cox," she says. "I was last in line."

He aims around himself a mole's assessing squint, suddenly exposed to light. "No line left, Sissy."

"But there was."

He assents, "I guess there was. You may as well take advantage."

"That's exactly it, Mr. Cox."

"What's exactly what?"

"If I came to you, I'd be taking advantage." She nods to the wall of wanted posters, but she means the men, and he knows she means the men.

Mr. Cox looks mole-ishly amused. "Did you see my trees, Sissy?"

"They're great trees. I like dogwoods. You did all of that?"

"Nobody else was about to," he says sourly. She has offended him. With Mr. Cox it always happens so fast. Where she has offended, Sissy has always felt an instant need to appease, and this, though nothing else would have, gets her to the counter, where she must hand over her letter to her mother, aware, suddenly, that she is being watched. She examines the backs of the silent men from the corner of her eye. One is leaning against the counter, not having removed himself as far as the others from her exchange with Mr. Cox. Rafer said that one of the migrants speaks a wary but quite good English, and stays by the counter all day, using the post-office pen on its chain of chrome beads to fill in the money-order forms for the others, who speak only Spanish. Rafer guessed that in Mexico he had been a teacher. Now, though she is not absolutely sure she is right about who he is, she smiles, the smile divided lightly between Mr. Cox and the young migrant, and falling on no one. Mr. Cox, unbemused, gives an economic lick to her stamp, and strikes it onto the letter's corner with his fist. "In here all day," he says, leaving off the *I've been* because he knows she knows that, "I forget what English is supposed to sound like. This all you came in for, Sissy? *One* stamp? We have these with wildflowers on 'em. I got the first sheets and thought of you."

She shakes her head.

"I thought you'd like 'em," he complains. "See?"

"You're busy," she says, to remind him of the migrants' silence.

"Always am, Sissy," he says. "Don't let it fool you that there's usually nobody in here. Nice to see you. Did you like those trees of mine?"

"Very much," she says.

"Bueno hay," he says to the young teacherlike migrant. "Let's get this damn operation under way again, *que no?*"

The migrant fingers the glossy pen at the end of its chain and pulls a fresh set of papers near. "O.K.," he says politely. Mr. Cox squints at the migrant and the pen with mole-ish rue, his mouth shut grimly. Sissy senses he dislikes this day-long appropriation, by the young teacher, of U.S. Postal Service property.

. . .

Dead, the jackrabbit lies with its legs stretched out behind it and its chin pillowed on the leaf of a wild gourd, halting the trembling of that one wide, insect-frayed leaf, though the other leaves still rock along the rabbit's back and past its out-flung heels, showing here and there, within the pointed shadows the leaves cast against each other, the hot yellow trumpet of a flower. A bloody cowlick is hardening at the base of the rabbit's skull, and a stray ant searches the pads of its extended forefoot, where the claws indent the coarse fur in snug stitches, each claw a pale husk with a curved marrow of compacted dust grains. Joe shudders beside Sissy with the intensity of the effort required to *stay*; he yawns and begins to pant. Tears fall from his tongue straight to the ground, where the dust pops into craters quick as those holes that percolate in wave-wetted sand. His ears are laid back, his eyes anxiously narrowed in the guilty look of a dog who is waiting for a human to perform some minor but necessary task. She whistles, willing Joe to glance at her, but he continues to stare at the rabbit in the leaves. His sense of what is right is as severe and unswerving as his gaze: she cannot shoot something and leave it to the crows.

She squats to draw the rabbit out by its hind legs, the smudged leaf, as the rabbit's head slides from it, springing up with an injured jack-in-the-box wobble. She tears a leaf away and wipes the ants from the rabbit's fur, trying to get them all, because they're red ants, and can sting. For some reason, she is being gentle.

"All right, Joe." She stands, and bends for the .22. "Is that what you wanted?" He only yawns foxily and trots away, looking back just often enough to make sure they're still a pair, that he doesn't get so far ahead that she feels abandoned: she is a responsibility Rafer has left with him. They are roughly a mile from the pickup, which she left on the highway's shoulder, and to get there they will cross a pair of irrigation ditches separated by an expanse of eroded furrows and wild grass dyed a starchy, faintly pink tan by the summer. Joe leaps the first irrigation ditch with several feet to spare, then circles back and wades into the massed reflections of the cattails on the bank. He drinks noisily, water striders skating between his legs, and once he snaps at a dragonfly. Sissy crosses above him on a bridge that is a single rocking plank. She lays the rabbit on the far end, puts the gun down, and takes off her sneakers. The dark water folds itself around her ankles and her reflection melts downstream in idle zebra stripes. The wind makes all of the reeds on the bank bend together, into each other, with a sound like slapping. She arches her feet and spreads her toes as wide as they will go. She examines her freckled arms for fleas from the rabbit. She shot it out of the worst sort of boredom, because it sat up in the field in front of her when Joe wasn't in the way, and she is sorry for it now. The rabbit's eye made a neat brown marble of a target, smaller than a chip of glass in the arroyo wall. This is Sunday, and Rafer was supposed to have been home last night; so it is almost sure he will be coming in tonight, and she can beg pearly garden potatoes and carrots from her neighbor, and slice them for a stew.

When she lifts her feet out, they feel silky, as if with algae, though they're quite clean. Joe looks up, water running from his jaws and chest. She picks up the gun, lifts the rabbit, and hastily changes her grip: its legs have stiffened, and the hocks resist her grasp in knuckly points, like a pair of dice. Joe is out of the water and far ahead, not even troubling to look over his shoulder this time, and she doesn't even try to keep up. The rabbit's head swings, upside down, past the arched tips of dry grasses.

Cautiously, she avoids a prickly pear that has occupied the peeling basin of an ancient tractor tire; some of the prickly pear's pads are engraved with zigzags of tire tread. In front, Joe gives two short, sharp barks—of warning—as she moves into the deep cattails of the second ditch's bank. She comes out beside Joe, who is sitting quite still on the steep bank, and together they look down at the young migrant who has been bathing there. The man cups his genitals in his hands and stares up at her, amazed and wild. Only after a shocked silence does she remember the gun in her hand and the rabbit she holds by its heels. She lets the rabbit slide slowly into the reeds, which close over it, and then kneels in studied slow motion, still facing the migrant, to lay the gun behind her, within reach but on the ground. She stays like that, very nearly kneeling, very nearly at eye level with the man in the stream.

His eyes are large, his lips drawn away from his teeth in a fear so extreme it seems unreal to her. She tries to think whether she has ever really frightened, really terrified anyone in her life before, and knows that she hasn't—not like this, and not even close. A thin white shirt is pinned like a kite in the cattails behind him. He had wanted to keep it dry, or air his sweat from the cloth, and this is a revelation of his fastidiousness, of something as private as his nakedness. She loves the half-floating, half-sagging shirt. She shakes her head softly, meaning it as an apology to him. She wants to apologize for coming so suddenly through the reeds, for forgetting the gun, for the way Joe is watching him, a strict surveillance. For everything. He must have understood what she wanted, because he says—oddly, perhaps even ironically, but with a certain sweetness—"Mil gracias." It is a phrase she has always liked. A thousand is so many, so generous.

Then, startled at seeing what—distracted by his nakedness —she hadn't seen before, she is sure that she knows him, that he is the schoolteacher from the post office. It is so quiet that she can hear the water running between his thighs. "De nada," she says. It is nothing.

It isn't nothing. She has seen in his face how scared he was, and she watches the significance of this dawn on him. He bends forward until the water laps across his flat belly. It is a clumsy position, but his body to the chest is hidden from her. He is still cupping himself, under the water. She can see his hands dimly.

"Do you speak any English?" she says.

His hair is dripping into his eyes, and he no longer wishes to look at her; it is as if he has an answer, and is deliberately withholding it. She likes the clean line of his cheekbone, the gravely downcast glance, but there is something mocking and set about his dark upper lip, where the mustache is a feathery trace. He looks over his shoulder to his shirt. She understands that this means she should now back away; she should let him get his shirt. She almost wants, so silently instructed, to do so, yet she wants—it is so exquisitely clear what she wants that she can't, for the fraction of an instant, condemn herself for wanting it—to watch him rise from the water.

Joe releases them from the game of statues. He laps noisily from the ditch and sniffs at the young migrant, who holds out his hand shyly. Joe ignores the hand. It is tipped up slightly, the fingers curled and at ease, the palm a grid of old cuts, some healed, others healing. The man begins to make coaxing noises, musical little whimpers. Coins of light reflected from the current float over his dark shoulders like minute spotlights. His chest, when he extends his arm, is adazzle. He smiles to himself at the dog's stubbornness. She knows that he will never, if he can help it, look at her again. He knows something is wrong with her from the way she is just standing there, but he doesn't know what it is, or how to free himself of her.

"You could talk to me if you wanted," she says. "Please? *Por favor?* You don't understand. I've heard you talk. I know you."

She tries to think if there is anything else she can say. There isn't. There simply isn't. She doesn't know any more Spanish. The man in the stream whines gently, like a dog.

That night, to make up for having been gone longer than he'd warned her he would be, and for whatever else it is that is wrong (something is), Rafer drives her the forty miles north to Cheyenne for a movie. She watches the taillights of the car before them blink and elide into the corner of his eye like a tear swept sideways by the wind. Then the red light vanishes and his eye is clear and dark until another set of taillights appears in it. She wonders where, in the unlit fields stretching away from the highway, the young migrant is, and what his life will be like after this. Rafer takes her hand in the dusk of the theater before the movie begins, rubs their two sets of knuckles along the armrest, and whispers, "This was a long way to come for a movie. You ought to feel properly grateful," and though for a moment she is, she does feel that, she whispers back, "Daddy, I want a bus ticket to L.A."

《 Faux Pas

Kyra was a transparent liar. She said, "I hate myself for having to run home," and her tongue touched the corners of her mouth, as it invariably did after lies, in a tic she was sure her five-year-old son noticed, but never her husband, Charlie, and never her English lover of the last six months, Brian. To whom she was lying now, adamantly yet without heat. She knew not to invest a lie with heat; the truth was so seldom invested with it. In fact she was willing, even anxious, to catch a taxi once this dinner of Brian's was eaten and over with, because it would mean she was honoring a promise she had made to herself, and then set herself strictly to keep. Although Charlie had taken Nicholas away, with another American father and son, to visit Stonehenge—which meant they'd be gone through tomorrow, late—she would not spend the night in Brian's flat. She did not spend nights with Brian, that was the promise, and she wouldn't this time, though it presented the perfect occasion, because she believed she'd be yielding more than a night if she stayed. She would be permitting some irreversible erosion of her real life—

her life with Charlie—or of her sense of the inevitability of her life with Charlie. They had been together since Charlie was a senior at the University of Michigan, she a shy, green-eyed sophomore. Though to Kyra her unfaithfulness had lately seemed the essential fact of her existence—she had thought Charlie could surely read it in her guilty, radiant face—Charlie remained an innocent. She meant for that innocence to save them, and she had hemmed it about with nervous protective strategies. That morning, Charlie had left home in a state of high excitement; he was far more entranced than his son by the idea of standing Druid stones.

Home was in this case across London, and not America, though New York was where she and Charlie and Nicholas would be before the month was out. For Kyra, that return flight was running away as well as running home, and she was relieved to have it looming so close. Charlie's company had wanted him to spend a year in London. For more than half that year, she'd been seeing Brian, and had proved unable to extricate herself from the affair. The flight would have to do it for her. She considered his cropped English head with new pity.

Pity was lost on him, as her lie-betraying tic had been, because his back was to her. In his cold kitchen with its floor of black and white tiles, the kind of cheap tiles that (Kyra now knew) were in kitchens all over London, Brian put the kettle on and shook olive oil into a saucepan, finding only two gold drops. He answered, "Right," either to what she'd said or to finding the tin empty. "Right" was a word covering numerous disappointments and afflictions with rueful adroitness; it struck her that she'd heard it too easily, too often, from him. It was disturbing that though the weight of her accumulated refusals— to say she loved him, to listen seriously to his sketchy plan for coming to New York next summer and working there—was very great, and though in addition she'd just lied to him, he was not going to catch her out. They were not going to quarrel, though lines from the quarrel they were not going to have floated through her head.

He whistled, his signal that he wanted her attention. He believed her to be a great daydreamer. In this belief he was, as he so often was, several shades too kind, or too unobservant, in his assessment of her. She set her wineglass down and went to the window in a halfhearted attempt to provoke. She liked it: a second-story window in the house he'd lived in for years. It looked out over a part of London still unknown to her. He lived not far from the river. The neighborhood's light was changeable, its houses small, and he knew it inside out. The cold evening had gone a slate blue that was steady even through the rain, which had swept in, darkening the indifferent brick backs of the closely built houses, their roofs aslant with a uniform steepness, and their drenched, coal-black gardens long since cleared and spaded.

Brian stood behind her and observed, of the rain, "Stairroddy," so that when she looked again the rain sliced down in ranked, vertical lines, domesticated and English. Tidy, she thought. On their single fugitive trip into the country, she'd laughed at a petrol station sign, KEEP BRITAIN TIDY, and he hadn't known why she was laughing. After that, a current of small misunderstandings and wrong interpretations had seized them, though she was conscious that they were both willing it away—their mutual incomprehension. It had not quite deserted them, even when the brief trip was over.

"Coming?" He was persuasive, interrupting her. He was going for more olive oil, and if she said no he would finally be hurt, though he wouldn't show it. He wanted every minute of her that he could get this evening, which he'd been anticipating a long while; it was improvident, and therefore unlike him, to have overlooked the olive oil, thus opening an inconvenient gap in the time when he'd meant to keep them sealed together.

She shook her head. "Your cold," she said vaguely. "Don't get wet."

She stayed where she was. At the front door's slam, pleasure bloomed, the intense, rare pleasure of being alone in his flat. Once or twice before when he'd gone out, leaving her here, she'd imagined going through his things, his books and letters and the pockets of his shirts. The idea of carrying out this rapid, furtive search left her with a sense of being almost erotically privileged and secure with him, as if it were something he'd allow her, when in fact he never would. He was far too private, too neatly, self-sufficiently English, for that. It had certainly not occurred to him that she'd even contemplate a thing so alien. Stolen insights: those were American. He gave her, of himself, what he wanted her to know. It wasn't that what he gave her was insufficient in any way, it was only that he did, in fact, give it. She got nothing from him covertly, not even in lovemaking. By now she believed she could only be satisfied by those truths about himself he would somehow, sometime, unwittingly grant.

The ring of fluorescence on the ceiling flickered, its icy white blinked on the porcelain finish of the stove and the crockery in the sink, and Kyra was alone in a kitchen she suddenly disliked: it represented the entire balked, failing evening, and when was she going to get home? She gave in to him, caught up her things, and ran down the dark stairs. Outside, there was rain in her eyelashes, rain in her hair, and rain to breathe, bearing its sooty smell of washed London pavements and alleys. Far down the street, seen from behind, with his worn Levi's, scuffed leather jacket, and close-cropped fair head, Brian could have been a rough American kid, even a gang member. This was a London ideal, and an illusion he spent some effort perpetuating: as she ran after it, it charmed her. The illusion was ruined by his huge, black, old man's umbrella. *He* charmed her. Half turning, not quite stopping, he dealt her one brooding look before he consented to own her again. They'd begun drinking while he prepared to cook, and in the resonant shelter of the umbrella she was suddenly drunk. Not noticing, he wound her black cashmere muffler again and again around her throat. Then they ran.

The shop was dim inside, and cluttered, owned by a slender, vigilant Indian who at once adopted an air of injury, as if they had interrupted him at something crucial. If Brian hadn't sometimes insisted, Kyra would never have entered the store after the first time, when the Indian's dislike of her was so eerily strong in the little coffee-fragrant box of a shop. Brian had an explanation: the shock of leaving India for this battered brown corner of London caused the Indian to detect in even the most everyday shifts and transitions in the lives around him a magnificent destruction. Appearing relatively recently, Kyra represented change, and therefore loss. She resented this nimbly expedient apology for someone's very visible dislike of her. Now, behind his counter, there was the Indian with his crimped black hair in waves over his delicate forehead, his long, feminine eyes taking her in with crazy hatred. With Brian's umbrella no longer over her head, sanctioning her presence, she was too exposed, too uneasily foreign for the frugal English smallness of the shop. It wasn't quite clean, and it was painfully quiet. She pretended to sort through the ice cream in the tiny freezer, but its interior was deep with drifted rime that seemed weirdly dusty, and she was disgusted. On the shelves there were the thrifty British sizes of everything: dwarf packets, toy tins, set out in grudging display, one or two of each.

"Daydreaming?" Brian said. He had got the oil. He bumped her out the door before him. She directed a late, languishing smile over her shoulder at the Indian, to confuse him. In the veiled shop darkness he appeared to be in pain. "What are you up to, child?" Brian demanded, but before she could answer there was someone standing near them, under an umbrella of her own, but facing them, facing, particularly, Brian, who was startled into tongue-tied stillness. Kyra stared. This was a way she'd never seen him before. It displeased her greatly.

"Um, Brian," the woman said.

"Pippa."

Pippa, Kyra thought drunkenly, excitedly, displeasedly. Pippa was Brian's ex-lover, and the last person in London he'd have wanted to run into with Kyra tonight.

"This is Kyra," Brian said. He sneezed.

Pippa said politely, "Kyra, hallo," offering her hand. Kyra shook it. The three of them, under two umbrellas, stood very still.

"Since I've run into you," Pippa said to Brian, "I wonder if I might come round to pick up some of my things."

"Some of your things? There's nothing of yours."

"There is something I can't find now, and I think I know where I left it."

"I haven't seen it."

"Um," Pippa said. "That's the awkward thing. You wouldn't have done."

Kyra's nervousness was growing. She tried to think why, and couldn't; this was an ordinary enough conversation. The decisiveness with which Pippa pronounced "awkward" was lovely.

"What was it, then?" Brian said.

"My black jeans."

She hadn't wanted to confess that, because jeans, taken off, proved intimacy, setting up a little echo of past sex, hers with Brian. She'd been being discreet for Kyra, though she had no idea who Kyra was.

Pippa had beautifully cut fair hair that fell over one of her eyes. There was a tiny mole near the corner of that eye, as well. Her muffler was wound again and again around her throat, and her fine nose was chapped with a cold the match of Brian's. She and Brian had moved nearer, their umbrellas cambered together to form this leakless, seamless black silk gloom, which shed rain only at their backs. Kyra was sure neither of them had given a thought to this positioning. Of their own accord, the umbrellas had lodged together into their old conversational fit.

"They're not there," Brian said, indignant.

"Brian, they are. You couldn't know they're not."

Because of the mole near the corner of her eye, or because she didn't know who Kyra was, Pippa's gaze wasn't absolutely candid. Through her drunkenness, Kyra began to feel slightly unreal, thinking how often, in the brief time they lived together, they must have met up like this, one coming, one going, with stray details of their small, tidy, hateful household to discuss. Dinner, tea. Biscuits, tickets. Pippa was an actress. She'd appeared in Brian's first play and in two of his plays since; even, Kyra knew, in the play that had overlapped and partly caused their breakup. Though drawn-out, that had been an Englishly gentle dissolution. Kyra had had no reason to expect what she now saw: in the needling downpour, confronted by Pippa, Brian had entirely lost his self-possession.

He had unconsciously edged Kyra toward the umbrella's rim, and her shoulder was getting wet, but it was Pippa who noticed. "Brian, you brute," she said, and with a finger tipped his umbrella farther over Kyra's head. "She's getting quite drenched."

Pippa and Kyra locked glances and laughed. "Thoughtless monster," Pippa added, to Brian.

"If you're serious, Pippa, then come," he said. "Let's get out of the wet."

Absolutely not, Pippa, Kyra rehearsed for him silently. *There's no way you can stop by tonight. You see, this is my American lover. We never have the luxury of an entire evening together.*

Pippa fell behind, but not far enough so that Kyra could

question Brian: What about dinner, how long would she stay? Kyra glanced back to determine if Pippa minded lagging behind the two of them, an unknown American and Pippa's own ex-lover, but Pippa was nonchalant, her gaze caught by each shining shop window they passed. At the house, a tomcat was sheltering in the recess of the front door, his torn ears flattened in annoyance at the relentless drumming-down wetness of the world. Pippa scooped him up and rubbed his big head against her chin until the cat broke into a purr. She dropped him, and they all three climbed the stairs, Brian and Pippa both hooking their umbrella handles over the bannister. The suspended umbrellas flopped open enough to dry, dripping on the floor below. Upstairs, Pippa paused to peer into the kitchen, and said, "Brian, you left the kettle on. It's all boiled away. You'll be burning the house down next."

"We didn't mean to stay away so long."

"Shall I start another?"

"Yes, please," Brian said.

So they would be bound together until tea could be completed. Dinner was nowhere in sight. Kyra said, "I think it's time for my taxi, Brian."

"Oh, no, impossible," Pippa said. "I've ruined your evening by running into you, haven't I? By coming up? Look, this is simple but it is awkward." Lovely "awkward" again. "Brian, I need to get into the bedroom."

"Bedroom," he repeated, and she nodded, her fair hair in her un-candid eye. They went into the bedroom, Kyra following.

"This *will* seem odd," Pippa said. "I can only say that I forgot." She bent over the bed, gave the mattress a twist that exposed the box spring, and tugged out a pair of slim black denim jeans. "You did like shortcuts," Brian said. She laughed. "Did, and do." She folded the black jeans and clasped them to her chest, under her chin, as she had cradled the cat. "I wish you'd ask me to tea," she said, yearningly. "Then I wouldn't feel

I'd made such a terrible *faux pas.* I did intrude. But you know"—
she turned abruptly to Kyra—"or you don't know, I lived here,
and it made things very strange for me, the feeling that I'd left
something here, and not only here, but, um, in the bed."

"They were quite safe here," Brian said. "They could easily
have remained where they were for years." From his neutral
tone Kyra couldn't tell whether he was teasing Pippa or whether
it was an oblique rebuke, but whichever it had been, Pippa
absorbed it in silence, as well as the fact that she wasn't going to
be asked for tea. She and Brian kissed good-bye, but this was,
Kyra guessed, from a need to stamp their accidental meeting
with the companionable finality, the leaving of no doubts in
anybody's mind, that had characterized their breakup. Pippa
nodded sweetly to Kyra and then, as if suffering a rush of doubt
or regret, extended her hand again, said, "Very nice meeting
you," and went.

"This is awkward, but I would *so* like some tea," Kyra said.
An impulse to mock Pippa as cruelly as possible had overcome
her, though she was certain no cruelty of hers would be enough
to twist Brian from his mood. Besides, her mimicry was im-
perfectly pitched. It sounded American and almost admiring. She
began again. "That was strange."

"Right," Brian said. "That was strange."

"You're repeating things. She started you doing that."

"What does it matter?"

"It matters like this: I've never seen you so thrown."

He sat on the edge of the bed and idly straightened the
duvet, which had been rumpled at the mattress's lifting.

She said, "I've never thrown you like that."

"Haven't you." He punched the duvet. Then he leaned
forward and put his face into her stomach, coughed hoarsely,
and said loudly enough so that she could feel his voice res-
onating through her belly to her backbone, "You have. You
do all the time. You change your mind, and you act as if I

haven't even noticed it, as if you have an absolute right to reverse yourself, even where it involves my deepest feelings. As if I should learn to exist without expectations. I'm cheated of what I would feel if I could trust you more completely. You know you *lie* to me."

She knelt, instinctively wishing to bring her face nearer his. He was finding it hard to meet her carefully fixed and tender stare of comprehension. He said again, though not as loudly, "You lie."

But looking up at him she saw he loved her nonetheless, and she forgot that she wasn't at home.

Black
Holes

Juniper and Jade Clark, who are twins, hog the windows in the station wagon's back seat, so that Fanny Giles, unwilling to climb over Jade's legs to get to the middle, is stranded for a moment on the school sidewalk. "Get in, Fanny," Mrs. Clark coaxes from behind the steering wheel. "Don't be shy." She leans forward and squints until she can see Fanny, whose red hair, backlit, has been drawn into a severe French braid that makes her small, sharp face even smaller and sharper; the wan, nutmeg freckles are so numerous that there are even stray flecks between the spikes of her lower lashes. Her upper lip has the dusty cast peculiar to light redheads, but her eyes are dark, and the wings of her nostrils pinkened as if by a cold. Looking at Fanny, Mrs. Clark thinks two things: Fanny is scared, and Fanny's mother must have been a fox.

"That's not shy," Jade says. "That's stupid. Climb in, Fanny-Panny. Nobody's going to tell on you. That's the rule of the car pool."

"Tell what?" Mrs. Clark says, as Fanny works her way into the seat. "No, don't tell me. I don't want to know."

"Oh, God!" Jade says. Fanny has nicked Jade's leg with the corner of her lunchbox, and a small hole blooms in the knee of Jade's black tights.

"No profanity in this car, not while I'm driving," Mrs. Clark says. "I don't care what your father lets you get away with."

Juniper breathes a cloud across her window and writes "ADAM." Jade, after glancing over her shoulder, fogs her window and writes "ADAM LOVES JADE." Juniper makes tongue prints; Jade draws a dozen deft Xs for kisses. Caught between them, awed by the twins' cold second-grade glamour, Fanny feels herself whittled down to a ragged scarecrow—a scarecrow with a note, weighing like lead in her pocket, that her kindergarten teacher asked her to take home. When Mrs. Clark brakes the station wagon abruptly and faces Fanny, Fanny wishes she could either disappear or turn into one of the twins, who are paying no attention to their mother.

"Hey, Fanny," Mrs. Clark says. "That's your new house, isn't it?" and points. Fanny looks up a sweep of gopher-pocked lawn to the house, its long porch trimmed with weathered gingerbread; there is a pane missing in the window to the left of the front door. Fanny nods yes.

"So?" Mrs. Clark says.

"So?" Jade echoes, absently mocking her mother, then writing on her window, "BORING!!"

"So do you think you'll like living there, Fanny?" Mrs. Clark persists. Juniper erases her window with the heel of her hand. "Suppose she doesn't, what's she going to do about it?"

"I like it," Fanny says softly.

"We're going to miss you," Mrs. Clark tells her, releasing the hand brake and letting the station wagon roll through the intersection. "We'll miss coming home from school with you."

"I won't," Jade says.

Biting her lower lip to concentrate, Juniper writes in the fog on her window, "Help!"

⟨ Saturday morning, Will Giles blows the blue-black husks of
⟨ dead flies from the channel in the window sash before gently pressing the new pane of glass into place. His reflection slants across it—a dark-haired man on his knees, looking hopeful. The glass fits, and the panes of the tall sidelight to the left of the front door are complete. He smiles over his shoulder at Fanny, who is sitting on the porch railing swinging her heels, and then he knocks on the door. "In a week, you'll be inside, and maybe you'll hear someone knock, and you'll feel nice and safe because you know whoever's there is knocking on solid oak. Isn't it a great front door, Fanny?"

Fanny is five, child of a marriage Will thinks of, with a blitheness he would immediately distrust in one of his analysands, as well forgotten. In fact, he has a recurring dream that he is in a booth trying to find enough change to call Oklahoma City, where Ally has lived since the divorce. Ally didn't think it very likely that she would keep in touch with Fanny—Ally didn't want anything that reminded her of her previous existence.

Fanny is rocking on the railing, one leg cradled to her chest, the knee tucked under her chin. He reaches for a screwdriver and taps her foot with it. "Hey, you look a little precarious."

"I can sit like this hours and not fall."

"Don't be so hard on my heart, Fanny."

She straightens, going as primly alert as if an invisible book has descended to her head, and carefully squeezes first one dirty sneaker, then the other, into the narrow gaps between the spindles that support the railing, daring him to tell her not to do that, either; when he doesn't, she looks faintly satisfied, and locks her feet, toed in, around the peeling spindle.

"Thank you," he says. "Once this is finished, your house is going to be in good shape." Since she's been coming here with him on Saturdays, he has taken to calling this her house. A truer joke might be that for a long time to come this is going to be the bank's house. His second wife, Carrie Ann, had argued that they couldn't keep Christopher's bed at the end of the hallway for long, that a baby and a five-year-old really need a room each. This costly Victorian, with its leaks and loose shingles, with swallows' nests suspended in its sooty chimneys, was her solution. Will is not in love with it, not the way his wife is, but he has begun to feel for it that involuntary affection sparked in him by things badly in need of repair.

"I thought there was still lots of stuff to do," Fanny says.

He begins to limn the new pane with the tube of glazing compound. "No," he says. "This is the last thing I wanted to get to"—and feels pleased and provident, having timed the last urgent repair for the last Saturday before they move in.

She jumps from the railing and slides by him, leaving the door half open. With a razor blade he trims a gauzy line of glazing compound into a neat margin, pausing now and then to admire the door, which, because a shaft of sun has now crossed the porch, blazes: old oak with its curls and knots and close grain, the gold hidden within the somber wood like flakes of precious metal in a stream, cartwheeling to the surface in certain lights, subtly lost from it in others.

He finds Fanny in an upstairs room that smells of drafty wallpapered emptiness, her chin on the windowsill, flaking scabs of paint away. Peels of paint lie on the sill and the floor. "Hey," he says. "You didn't swallow any of those, did you?"

She shakes her head, chin pivoting on the sill, her nose nearly touching glass. "I don't eat paint," she says, with dignity.

"I think about things like that, *chico*. I'm a father." He sits in a corner, deciding from her silence that she should have his entire attention. Since Christopher was born, he has too often found he had nothing left over for Fanny, though he has sworn that would never happen. "So how are you?" he says. "How's school been?"

To his surprise, she pulls a folded slip of notebook paper from her pocket. "My teacher said I had to give you this."

"What is it?"

"I can't read writing yet. Only printing." She drops it to the floor.

He picks it up and begins to refold it, creasing it into an airplane. Should he open the window and let it fly? "But you didn't like the idea of giving it to me?"

"I was going to. I was waiting."

He tucks the airplane into a pocket, walks to her on his knees, and waits for her to turn her head, but she doesn't; at arm's length, she is so still he can hear pigeons walking on the wooden shingles over their heads. "Tell me something, Fan," he pleads. "Have I seemed far away lately?"

"No."

"Because I want you to know you can always find me. Have you felt, maybe, that it's been hard to get my attention?"

"You're just you."

"Yes," he says, "but is that good or bad?" He pretends the end of her braid is a paintbrush and traces the corner of her mouth with it. "No answer, huh?" He tickles under her pale jaw until she has to smile. He says, "I can see you want me to fear the worst."

"Fanny's in a little trouble at school," Will tells his wife from the bedroom doorway. He has been prowling the lawn, as he does when he is uneasy, pulling up dandelions. Before marrying for the second time, he had tried to think it all through from Fanny's perspective, hoping to anticipate where the dangers for her would lie: he had come to the conclusion that there was another sort of risk, perhaps less immediately obvious, in her feeling that she had been responsible for keeping him from marrying again, and that in neither condition, married or unmarried, could he absolutely guarantee her safety. Yet he hates saying "Fanny's in a little trouble" so much that for an ominous moment he dislikes everything—past, present, and opalescent future; first wife, long gone, and second wife, regarding him sleepily; this house and the forlorn, mortgaged Victorian. In the bed, Carrie Ann wakes enough to turn her cheek to the baby's round forehead and direct her dark gaze, made darker by dilating pupils, at her husband, disliking him back in a rudimentary but very effective form of self-, and baby-, defense.

"She brought home a terrible note," Will says.

He rubs a knuckle against the door latch, meaning *Is this loose?*; it is not. Carrie Ann, thrusting two fingers into the Pampers, smiles to find the powdered bottom dry; these simultaneous small discoveries dissolve the anxiety between them. Will continues to click the latch, but now simply for the sound it makes, and because he likes latches, locks, lintels, dowels, and bolts.

"Fanny in trouble?" Carrie Ann fits the tip of her pretty nose into Christopher's ear, and he opens his eyes and looks questioning. So often the mood of one is either a premonition or a minutely lagging echo of the mood of the other.

"Nothing too serious."

"But *some*thing."

"Something," he agrees, and is halted by the intentness of the baby's nearsighted stare. Carrie Ann cups the back of the baby's head so that he seems a bald, bewildered old man gazing at the doorway. He has no eyebrows. "You should see him from here," Will says. "He looks like Einstein thinking about ice cream."

Carrie Ann licks the nearly invisible down above the perfect, almost comically precise, ear. Then, alternating licks with shaping strokes for which she uses the inside of her wrist, she flattens the tufts at the crown of the head. A fist floats her way, opening into a starfish of sticky fingers, each one of which she sucks in turn, causing—Will can see it, though she can't—the corners of the mouth to turn down in sober baby pleasure, the peak of the upper lip to glisten. Until the amniocentesis, Will had been frightened because he wanted the baby so badly, yet believed in spite of himself that something would turn out to be wrong. He had urged the test on Carrie Ann, who was thirty-two, though her obstetrician didn't recommend amniocentesis until the woman was thirty-four. Once they knew the baby was all right, and that it was a boy, Carrie Ann mused through the rest of the pregnancy, talking to her belly, praising its kicks. What Will sometimes wonders is: Did the baby—or fetus—forgive him, and did he do something he ought to be forgiven for? He finds it interesting that the first question always precedes the second, and whenever he attempts phrasing them to himself in the more logical order, they resist. They freeze exactly where they are.

Now when Will gets up in the night and pads down the hallway, the baby sometimes tries to nurse from his father's chest (is that forgiveness?), the corky nipple, hidden within a whorl of dark male hair, hardening helplessly as the hungry vacuum fastens upon it, and remaining there, stinging slightly between the silky gums, until the baby exhales it with a sigh of disappointment. The baby's head makes a snug, familiar fit in Will's left hand, its back a lax weight along the tendons of his forearm, and he rocks Christopher close to his chest down the long unlit hall. Once, half asleep, he caught himself whispering, "It's me. It's me. Me," to the small face.

He was far too young, too unsure of himself, to be so available when Fanny was born. There is a little scene that unreels now and then in his mind: Fanny, her chin in her palm, telling her psychiatrist how distant her father was, how she could never seem to reach or please him, and her psychiatrist nodding gloomily. For some reason, Will finds this fable of the future reassuring. Perhaps it is because the (twenty? nineteen-year-old?) Fanny is beautiful, or because psychiatry is his profession, and she has turned to it, which would seem to imply she hasn't rejected him completely. It's not as if, in his mind's eye, she is without hope. So now he rattles the latch again and lets the paper fall to the quilt. "You're not going to like it," he warns.

Dear Dr. and Mrs. Giles:

It's with some hesitation that I write to you. (Ordinarily, we ask parents to come in, but I know how busy you must be with a new baby.) I am also aware that a new baby in the household is a real test for everybody and the older child may be left on her own more often, especially a child like Fanny, who has so many resources of her own. It's because Fanny is such an achiever that her recent unwillingness to participate in class discussions, and her confusion when called on, strike me as worrying. She has also been responsible for a series of small thefts: a paperweight belonging to another girl, and some other little things, were found in her coat pockets. No one has accused her of stealing—a five-year-old barely understands the word.

None of these things are important in themselves, but they may be symptoms of some deeper problem, and I wondered if you'd be interested in having Fanny talk to our school counselor, Mr. Yatsumoto?

Best wishes, and congratulations,

Delia Dorsey

"What a bitch," Carrie Ann says. "Delia Dorsey. What a funny mix of accusation and flattery this is. I think this entire letter is evidence of a truly dull mind at work. I mean, it really depresses me to think that Fanny has fallen into her hands." Christopher mews for her breast. She rakes up her T-shirt and lets the breast descend. "She'll see Mr. Yatsumoto over my dead body."

"You know," Will says, "I thought the one thing wrong with moving was that Fanny will have to change schools."

"I hate this," Carrie Ann says, reading over the baby's head. " 'Responsible for a series of small thefts.' If only someone like Delia Dorsey had been around to finger the young Richard Nixon, we'd never have had to go through Watergate and be disillusioned as a nation. She obviously doesn't know the first thing about Fanny. Do you want to know one reason I fell in love with you so fast? Because you were alone and yet you had this bright, serious, *serious* little girl, and I thought, He must be doing something right."

"Not anymore, I'm not." Will lies down on the bed with the interesting sensation that he is trapping Carrie Ann, keeping her in place, because she is under the quilt and he is on it. The baby's head doesn't turn, though his temple pulses with the quick, small sucks that have drawn the nipple into his mouth. "In fact, I must be doing something pretty wrong. Haven't you noticed a change? Fanny's almost stopped confiding in me. That's never happened before."

Carrie Ann strokes his forehead and he smells baby on her wrist. "Oh, Will, maybe it was time for it to happen."

"I don't believe that."

"Some things are inevitable, but you don't believe that, either, do you?"

"I think believing that is a way of giving in," he says.

"If I think about it too long, I'm going to get really furious at Delia Dorsey and Mr. Yatsumoto, and then my milk will stop."

He stands up, the mattress creaking. "I'm going," he says. "We can't have your milk stopping."

"Will?"

He is in the doorway. "What?"

"Now I feel guilty."

"Don't feel guilty," he says.

{ On Fanny's quilt, pink with indigo stars of eight points each, Will turns on his side and sings into her hair,

> "The fox went out on a dreary night
> And he prayed for the moon to give him light—"

"Stop," Fanny says. "I don't like that anymore."

"You don't?" He pretends astonishment, thinking astonishment is what she wants, but really he is used to things changing fast. She has never been one for the same fairy tale night after night. "How about another song?"

"No."

"Want to read *East of the Sun, West of the Moon?*"

"No. Dad?"

"Nnnnn-nh?" He loves her hair: fine, red-gold, kinky, the neat part white as bone and so sweet-smelling. Adult hair was never like that.

"How far is it from here to my house?" Fanny asks.

"Not so far." He remembers a story a patient told him— how the patient's daughter had been struck with grief because the family's battered old Volkswagen was about to be sold. "You mean you'd like to come back sometimes and see this place?"

"Can't I, if I want?"

"Look. This star on the quilt is the new house, see? Then

you go around the corner, take the first left, go straight one, two, three blocks, then you turn right, like this"—he walks it with his fingers—"and bingo, there's our house. Does that seem too hard to remember?"

"No."

"Don't worry, you'll get it. You're a quick study, *chico*."

"I am?"

"Sure. It's a pleasure to tell you things because you get them so fast."

"What happens if you're wrong?"

"If I'm wrong about what?" he says.

"What if I never really learned the things you were telling me? What if I forgot them all?"

"All? You wouldn't forget them all. Some knowledge you're born with. You have your mother's sense of direction." A rule long abided by: praise her mother to her as often as possible, in particular when praise is due. He points to the quilt. "This is the new house. You're here. Now you walk it."

She walks her fingers around the first corner, follows the pink for three blocks with a precision that almost kills him, and is getting warm when he catches her hand and swallows it to the knuckles, making devouring noises. "I forgot," he says around her fingers, "to warn you about the black hole in between. Mmmmmmm, nnnnnh, how good you are, delicious child, all gone."

To his astonishment, the gray eyes brim. He lets go of her hand. "What? Did that hurt?"

"No."

"I didn't think it was hard enough to hurt. Was it?"

"No."

"Are you worried about what the note said, then? Because I'm not."

"I know it."

"Then, Fanny?" She turns on her side, facing the wall, and he puts his cheek to her warm, small back. "Fanny?" Still no answer. "Fanny?"

At last she says, "What?"

"Can't you tell me what's wrong?" He feels all of his patience, professional and domestic, trained and intuitive, impartial and yearning, brought to the finest point of attention, his nose buried in the light flannel of her nightgown, his eyes closed, his heart hanging on her next word, which is:

"Nothing."

On Friday, after following Fanny through the new house, Will pretends he is blind and pats down the wall by the front door for the switch, missing it. A realtor, leading the way through one of the houses they considered, told him it takes nearly a month before you acquire that seemingly instinctive way of being able, in the dark, to put your hand directly on the light switch. The realtor seems to have been right. "Have you given any thought to where you'd like the telephone, Fan? The telephone guys are coming tomorrow, right in the middle of everything."

"Will you call?"

"Will I call?" Bemused, he locks the door behind them. She jumps to the railing, draws her knee to her chest, and begins to rock strenuously. A neighbor's cat is in the corner of the porch.

"Fanny, I've told you about that. Stop."

"Will you call?" The neighbor's cat comes close; with her bare foot, toes extended, Fanny strokes its head between the ears.

"From the clinic? I always call, you know that."

"You always used to."

"I don't get it, *chico*. Why's it going to be different?"

"What about," she says with an effort, "when I'm here, and they're there, *then* will you call me?"

"Who's they?"

"Carrie Ann," she says, "and the baby."

"So where are you, and where are they?"

"They're in your house," she says. "And I'm moved in here, tomorrow."

"Oh, *chico*," he says. "Is that what you think?"

She lets a foot rest lightly on the cat's head; delicately, with constraint, the cat yawns. "I know you have to have a house for just you and Carrie Ann and Christopher. I know you do. I like this house all right."

"Oh, Fan, no! No—it isn't that way at all. That was only a dumb joke, the way I kept saying that this house was yours. This house is for *all* of us to live in—we're moving out of the old house together, into this one. We're a family. We're a little bigger family than before because of Christopher, but we would never want to live apart from you. Never. We couldn't stand it."

The cat hooks a paw as if to scratch at Fanny's ankle, and only swats—swift, small, apprehensive swats, claws in.

"I'm not sure about that cat, Fan."

"That cat won't hurt me." In proof, the cat begins to purr, and turns its cheek to Fanny's callused heel, moving its head back and forth.

"Fanny?" he says. "It must have been so lonely for you."

Fanny stares at the cat. "Forget it," she says. "Just forget it, Dad."

⟨⟨ Carrie Ann puts the tip of her nose into Christopher's ear. She closes her eyes and inhales. Very dexterously, in his sleep, his fist opens and closes, closes and opens, thumb over fingers, fingers over thumb, in a way that is both delightful and monotonous to watch closely, the fist surrounding, and never quite releasing, some strands of Carrie Ann's hair. She lifts her mouth to Will for his kiss. When she turns her head, the strands caught in the baby's fist draw tight.

"How could she think up something like that?" she says. "It would never even have occurred to me that we needed to be on guard against Fanny getting an idea like that. How could you have possibly known she'd come up with something so farfetched?"

"It wasn't farfetched," he says. "It was reasonable, in its way. She was only listening to what I said."

She pats the quilt, signaling *Lie down*; he nods to the hall-way, meaning *I have to go talk to her some more.* Carrie Ann persists in patting the quilt: *I want to comfort you. Don't you need it, too?* So he does lie down, his body anchoring her body in place, and her foot, below the quilt, sliding slowly down the length of his calf above it. She whispers, so she won't wake the baby, "God, Will, you want to know something? I think it's just about the saddest thing that's ever happened in the world, don't you?"

Will puts his head on her shoulder. The baby between them, they lie staring at the wide shadowed ceiling. She giggles, and suddenly they are both shaking with soft laughter, quite silent, something neither son nor daughter will ever hear.

⫽ Favor

From around the corners of the house, from as far away as the orchard, hens shied into the yard, scurrying as they felt other hens behind them, then lagging back to feed. Two chesty matrons tumbled into a smaller black hen. She darted under a strand of wire, and when the old man turned, he could detect only her back in a fine mesh of grass shadow. She was getting wild, and Sandoval's mouth set in a hard line. He didn't want her to hide out all morning, but there was little he could do that wouldn't scare her more. He chided, "Damn cheeks, do I got all day? Leave that Lola alone. Doan go after her, now, you, or—"

He left the threat hanging over them as the hens, in a sudden gang, crowded forward. Sam looked up, startled; Lola had been the old man's wife's name. "That little one's Lola?"

Sandoval shrugged without troubling to glance Sam's way; a precise economy, long ago decided on, ruled even his movements. "Cheek, cheek-cheek, pretty cheek," he called to the black hen, his Adam's apple working as he clucked. The yard was bare except for some brierlike roses under the eaves, where the rain spilled in torrents after storms: his wife's roses, which he had clipped down cruelly after she was dead, as he pruned down almost everything too far, until there was little left to bloom. She had been seventy, and not five feet tall, and she used to come and put her body between those roses and him with his shears. Old Man Sandoval was a miser; he wanted nothing to yield too generously, too unthinkingly—worst of all, to give in such a way that he could not get his hands on what had been given and cunningly husband it. He dreaded the leaf-dappled, camouflaged clutch, the apple dropping into the irrigation ditch. He had never had any children.

On the woodpile, Sam cradled the old man's shotgun, broke it, and peered down the barrel. Snugged to his shoulder, the walnut of the long, trim stock had a bracing heaviness. The gun was a beauty, in mint condition, and it would be impossible to find another like it. Sandoval had lost a hen and a rooster, and he'd been telling Sam how it happened: from below the bedroom window had risen the reek of skunk, but when the old man tried to climb from bed his knee stabbed him with pain, and he had to lie there, staring at the ceiling, through the hens' ruckus. Sam missed the noisy banty rooster, Chico, with his rakish tail feathers, but when he tried to figure which of the hens was gone he couldn't; they were too alike to him, with their peckish feuding, and the only hen he recognized was Lola. Sandoval had brought the gun outside for Sam to examine, because tonight, Sandoval said, there would be a moon, and he was going to wait for the skunk in the rocks behind his henhouse, wait all night if he had to—an oath sworn as the old man bent and gingerly felt his knee.

Sam meant to try the gun in the arroyo behind his own house, but he was waiting until his wife, Jenny, a painter, would be in her studio, and no longer nursing a cup of her inevitable pitch-black coffee in front of their kitchen window. She was sure he did too many favors for the old man as it was, and she refused to admit any trace of Sandoval's charm. Last evening, Sam had come home, kissed her, and said, "Jen, I finally figured out why he props cardboard around his truck."

She wiped away the kiss, studying him with some dislike. "You figured out what?"

He steered her to a window. Below, in the far corner of Sandoval's yard, was the rust-spotted Chevrolet, with scraps of salvaged cardboard tipped to rest against it. "Did you ever notice that?"

"No. I never noticed that."

"Well, listen." He was still excited. "He props that cardboard up to protect his tires from the sun. He thinks it's going to make the rubber last longer."

"Oh, Sam, nobody could think that."

"He does."

"How do you know?"

"I just know. It was bothering me, and I figured it out. I'm getting to understand how he thinks."

He wanted to kiss her again, but she said, "I think that's so sad," and didn't say what was sad—the old man or Sam's wondering about him. Sam heard the rebuke: no insight into Sandoval's cunning would ever impress Jenny, she was so sure that time spent with the old man was another way Sam avoided repairs on their own house.

Their house: he hadn't predicted it would work as a wedge between them. At first, Jenny had handled the confusions of renovation fairly well, but before long the recriminations began. There were too many problems he hadn't foreseen, and she acted as if she should have been warned exactly how hard it was going to be. Sam could have prodded more skeptically through the house as a buyer, remarking its shortcomings and pretending to the real-estate agent that the sale could fall through, but he had been helpless—for Sam the house was love at first sight. The roof had proved to be dirt covering old, warped planks, glossed over by tar, whose bright black glister had falsely reassured him, when he climbed the ladder and leaned over the parapet, that the roof was sound. The tar had been new, but the dirt below it dampened with rain, and by November a strand of water, tinted red by the dirt, leaked across kitchen quarry tiles Sam had painstakingly laid. "The kitchen was the only room finished," Jenny said, "and now it's ruined"—though it wasn't, though a little water couldn't hurt quarry tile and butcher block, but Jenny, shaking the dirty pages of a sodden cookbook, refused to be comforted by the truth. A house in the country—there were always things wrong, he told her, especially with an old house, an unimproved house, a house they could afford: hadn't she known it would need patience? Lately she rarely bothered to argue, and he found her silences more disconcerting than quarrels—they never made love after a silence. He was a carpenter, a mender, a rescuer, and he hated knowing there was something wrong between them that he couldn't get at, and Jenny had let him live with that fact for the last edgy year. He wondered what he could try that he hadn't already; he could stay home more often, but the house oppressed him with the sense of things left undone. Originally, the house's imperfections had seemed an aliveness, even a rich-ness—part of its character, he would have said, and did say, in selling the house to Jenny. Those flaws turned against him, settling into grim, long-standing grudges, when he had meant to shoulder all burdens so handsomely, to tend to all the details before they could occur to Jenny as nuisances. Now, no matter how hard he worked, Sam seemed errant, and for Jenny his sunny afternoons spent in the old man's company were wasted, symptomatic of Sam's failure to be absolutely (inhumanly) re-sponsible. *Responsibility* is a favorite word of Jenny's lately, and *separation* is another. *You have no sense of,* and *Maybe we ought to think about.*

Sam lit a match and held it to a cigarette, though cigarettes were something he'd almost given up. Sandoval was hobbling across the yard, his fedora tilted to the back of his head, his unshaven jaw exposed to the sun. The edges of his eyes were red and inflamed, the lids sly and deeply arched. His hat and his breath both smelled old. He fished a cigarette from the bib of his overalls. Sam stood up for him, and they shared the match, and calmly smoked.

"I'll do it," Sam promised. "I'll get him for you."

{{ When the school bus stopped, Naranjos's blind mare hooked her big dusty head over the fence so the passing children could stroke her nose. Late last year Jenny and Sam's mailbox had been shot by someone driving by, and now that it was fall the wasps that were everywhere searching out niches had climbed in through the bullet holes. Sam sprayed the inside of the mailbox, slammed its door, and then he and Jenny ran. Wasps threaded out through the bullet holes and waited—a dozen wasps, two dozen, their abdomens jerking in rage.

"Is the wind this way?" Jenny asked. She didn't want to breathe it; she thought she was pregnant. She hadn't told Sam, though if he'd been anything except entirely self-absorbed he would have guessed it by now—she had even stopped drinking coffee. Last week, she'd taken the little jar into town, to her gynecologist's office, and he was supposed to call tomorrow morning early, but Jenny already knew what he would tell her. The wasps drifted from the mailbox; it was hard to tell if they were flying or had been blown away.

Sam said, "It can't hurt you. It hasn't hurt them."

To Jenny he sounded disappointed. "Maybe they'll come back and you can kill them over again."

This was cheering, and he agreed, "Maybe," swinging the

spray can as they walked back up the road, pausing for the old man, who was leaning against a tree; by the innocence in his face, Jenny knew they'd been ambushed. The tree was another thing that the old man had mutilated in pruning, but it appeared to have forgiven him, and bore apples in hard, small hundreds. There were none left now, and Jenny wondered where they'd gone; certainly he'd given few enough to them. She had a reason to like Sandoval, because he had signed the grant of easement that had finally cleared the title of their house to the bank's satisfaction, but her gratitude had been whittled away each time her husband disappeared to run the old man's errands.

Sam clapped Sandoval between the shoulder blades as he hunched over, coughing into a rag of handkerchief; he cleared his throat and croaked, "Good, good, *gracias, hito,*" as if his life had been saved.

You old actor, Jenny thought; you old cheat. *"Hito"* was a word that couldn't fail to move Sam, but all the affection went one way. It went from Sam to the old man. She leaned her cheek against Sam's back, so that he was between her and Sandoval, because sometimes she had the uncanny sensation that Sandoval knew exactly what she was thinking. His voice reverberating through his own shoulder, Sam told the old man what time to expect him tonight (What time to expect him tonight?), and Sandoval limped away through his dwarfed trees. Jenny knew he was old, he was alone, and it was wrong to resent whatever use he made of Sam, but Jenny knew a number of troublesome truths that seemed to have only negligible influence on her emotions. She knew it should be simple to make up with Sam, and she knew she had a very good reason to try, and she would—she would try, if only things between them hadn't locked into a pattern so stubbornly wrong, which had not, any of it, been her fault.

⟨⟨ The mattress rocked as Sam got out of bed, and, asleep, Jenny said, "What?"

"Me," he whispered into her hair. It took him annoyingly long to dress, because he needed warm work clothes and couldn't remember where they were. On the bureau he found a billed cap and tugged it on, and then he lifted long johns from the floor and, from a corner, Levi's that were both grass-stained and oily. There was something evil about pulling on cold, dirty blue jeans in the dark, he felt, but he needed clothes that wouldn't show against the night. He emptied his pockets of change—dime against dime could betray him to a wild thing.

From the bed, while he searched for his jacket, she asked, "Do you really have to kill something?"

"The old man's losing chickens, Jen."

"You don't want to."

"I'm not in love with the idea, no."

She got up, went down on her knees, and drew his jacket out from under a chair; he wondered what impulse of helpfulness this was. "Stingy old bastard," she said.

"Well, maybe." He shrugged into the cold denim, and found a glove.

"He is. Why do you have to go? Can't he find some nephew of his or something?"

"You know he can't."

She found his other glove, balled it up, and rubbed her upper lip with it. "What's this smell?"

She was naked; he liked her small, suspicious face. "Cloves. That's a hunting glove, it can't smell too human. Give it."

"He can't find anyone else because they all hate him. I hate him. You're never here."

"Back to bed." She obliged. It was like telling a fairy tale:

Sam said, "You're going to sleep again, nice and warm, and before you're up I'll be home. You'll think this was a dream."

The chill in the grass wet his sneakers as he trotted down the slope, across the road, into the weedy margin of the old man's orchard, through the still, small trees. A brier caught in his sneaker laces. Bending to pick it out, he found himself looking into the eye of a goose—whose?—worrying her own breast in deft, diving nips. Finished, she sleeked her cheek against brown feathers. They regarded each other so intently that when, nearby, an apple fell, Sam jumped. Coming out from the trees, he found the old man's kitchen lit.

Sandoval had laid the shotgun across the kitchen table. Sam liked the lamplight guttering across the rough adobe walls to the shadowed ceiling, and the warmth from the wood stove was nice, but he had to leave now if he wanted to do any good. He shook his head, from superstition, when the old man said, "You're gonna get him, I know." When the kitchen door latched behind Sam, the dark was darker; he'd lost his night vision.

At the henhouse he squinted through a chink, and though he could distinguish nothing inside, the hens continued their dovish burbling undisturbed. He clambered up the sandstone reef; his foot slipped, a pebble skipped away and struck, and down the valley a dog began to bark, waking another dog farther away. Sam climbed until he found the right shelf, wide enough to lie on, not too high for a good view. There was, for some reason, a rusty car fender lying on this shelf, and when he pushed it away its racket silenced the hens. He lay down flat, and as the stone chilled his stomach he concentrated on the smell of Jenny's hair, at that moment the most pleasant warmth he could come up with. He tried to work this warmth down to his fingers and freezing toes, but it remained in a ball in his chest. Below, nothing stirred, and the hens started in again. Sandoval's kitchen light blinked out, and Sam was glad, because it meant the old man trusted him enough to go back to bed. Or, he worried, it meant the old man was saving electricity, sitting waiting in the dark for Sam to succeed.

For an hour, then another, Sam lay counting alternately stars and the barks of distant dogs, guessing he would be able to spot in the grass the white chevron between snub ears, and wishing he felt better about killing the skunk. Lying there, he had begun to sympathize with it. The poor plank henhouse invited plunder, and the hens sounded idiotically cozy. Jaw to the shotgun's stock, Sam ran through his reasons. What he hated was the old man's sadness about his hens, and killing the skunk would put a stop to that. Fair enough—Sam was willing to take on this responsibility for that motive, and in his mind he had already neatly finished off the skunk's existence, leaving only the cold wait until he pulled the trigger. But the shape he finally observed, at the bottom of the reef, circling another rusty fender that lay there, moved nimbly, without a skunk's toed-in, tail-up shambling, and with many fractional hesitations and scent checks that were, to a skunk, quite unnecessary; what was coming through the cold green grass put its feet down briskly, kept its ears pricked and its tread light, and was, Sam saw, a fox.

Where the brush was deepest, the fox feinted in and out, keeping low, reluctant to show itself fully, but it was exposed as it skinnied under the fence and jumped to the henhouse ramp, where it paused. Its ears pointed forward, then back, and if Sam had whispered, the fox would have caught it. It sat, fitted its tail around its feet, and squared its shoulders silkily, as a hunting cat does for a bit of last-minute concentration—Jenny would have loved seeing that. The fox crouched, its ears angled now at the doorway, within which the hens were still foolishly burbling. Fox or skunk, Sam thought, the old man's loss was the same, and this death the end of his trouble. Sam made up his mind, a stone by his elbow chinked against another stone, the shotgun kicked into his shoulder, and the fox tucked into the doorway. The report echoed down the valley; Sandoval's kitchen went bright. Sam patted his jacket down for another shell, and cursed his confidence when he knew there wasn't one; he made the climb down sandstone, its cold grain scraping his hand. The hens sounded as if they were all dying bloody deaths, but by the time Sam had run to the henhouse door and knelt there, not even sure what he could do if he cornered the fox inside, he found only the fluttering hens, and feathers rocking down through shadow, and nothing else.

⟨ In the warm kitchen, Jenny said, "You missed because you ⟨ didn't really want to kill it." She was in her nightgown, making coffee, and she seemed very pleased with herself, with her own version of what had happened. "Was it beautiful?"

"Very. All sleek and fat from chickens. You should have seen the old man, Jen. He was so disappointed in me."

"Well, I'm not."

For once, he thought. "He couldn't believe I'd missed."

She surprised him: "That was hard for you, letting him down."

"He trusts me, Jen. I'm going to have to spend the afternoon wiring the henhouse up, so he can lock it right. It needs a new door."

"Not this afternoon, you can't."

"I have to fix the way the fox got under the fence as well. Why not this afternoon?" In spite of himself, he was irritated. Well, he'd been up half the night.

"We have to go into town," Jenny said.

"Why both?"

"Because I'd like it." Behind him, she scrubbed her chin along his denim jacket, with its night smell of faint cold grassy dustiness; he always seemed a little strange to her when he came back from hunting. She rubbed the hair at his neck, which needed a trim. She said, "My doctor called, and he says that I'm pregnant, but I've known that. I've just known."

His reaction to her words was physical—a startling in his chest, like alarm. He could understand the million metaphors and references to hearts, because that was where this happened. But he was quiet; misinterpreting that, she rushed on. "If only it wasn't such a rotten time for it, I know. If only we hadn't been having problems. I can't tell how I feel about a baby, Sam, can you?"

He meant to be cautious with her. He didn't want the answer he made now to be counted against him at any future time, to be entered into the list of his failures of intuition, and a part of himself was rapidly calculating and rejecting responses. She pushed his back. "Come on." She pushed harder. "Say something."

The part of him that answered her hadn't considered strategy at all; it was only guesswork, but Sam said, "I love you."

⟨ Wasn't there sometimes a period of grace, after you happened ⟨ to do something right, when you could do no wrong? When the old man had counted up his chickens and found them all there, when the fox didn't return, when Jenny brushed her hair singing, Sam guessed he had entered such a time, though a stray question from his former, troubled existence haunted him: If he had killed the fox that night, what would Jenny be like now? He knew what she would be like, and it wouldn't be good. He had come so close to killing the fox for the old man, and it would have proved to be, for Jenny, a kind of last straw. God, it was scary what he went through life not knowing.

But for now Sam believed he had pulled off an astonishing feat: he had got three—ah, four—lives into a kind of harmony.

. . .

{ It began to smell like snow, though there was no snow. It occurred to Jenny that there were things that had stayed undone since they had moved in which would still be undone when nine months were up—her baby would be born into an imperfect house, and this cost her some peace of mind. She stood before the house in the evening, filled with impatience. Outside, it was exactly as it had been for the last fifty years. The front of the house was eroding adobe, of a soft, quilted fawn, the same shade as the bluff that backed and appeared to shelter it. This bluff was the only thing Jenny unequivocally loved about the house. The separate bricks had weathered to a compact roundedness, all corners gone, and where the mortar had fallen out the facade buckled into a series of chinks, hollows, and inlets deeper than her fingers. In short, repairs were urgently needed, and Sam was gone again, down to Sandoval's yard, splitting kindling for the storm. The old man, Jenny knew, saved his gnarliest, hardest cedar for Sam.

She shrugged to herself, pulled her sweater higher around her throat, and cut down the slope to Sandoval's yard, where she sat on a bucket. The old man was sitting, too, not far from her bucket, but not near, either, and they nodded formally. Sam drove the wedge into a stump, extremely hard; the maul descended in heavy clops, again and again, and sometimes he let it fall and knelt to wrestle with the roots, trying to work them farther apart. The heartwood creaked like a saddle as the wedge inched deeper in.

"It's going to snow soon," Jenny said. "Can't you feel it?" She wrapped her arms around herself. Neither of them appeared to hear, but they were far beyond small talk. Sam had told her he thought he'd made the henhouse safe enough, and that the shot had surely terrified the fox. He'd told her, too, that the apples were in the old man's attic; sitting on her bucket, Jenny considered all that the old man would never, ever dream of giving away, and found she didn't care. She supposed that the way she thought of him now was the way Sam had thought about him all along—Sandoval was the way he was, and you had to accept him as that. Jenny was much more interested, now, in what was happening in herself.

It was colder, it seemed almost too cold to snow, and finally it snowed. Naranjos's blind mare slept under snow, and her furred nostrils left white vapor in the air. Jenny and Sam, returning home from a late movie in Santa Fe, saw the mare as they turned into their lane, and Jenny said, "Poor horse."

"Snow can't hurt a horse," Sam said. "It's probably warmer on her back than nothing." Brilliant light, low to the ground, prodded around the blind curve before them, and because it was hardly wide enough there for two vehicles to pass, Sam pulled onto the road's side, which was frozen hard. Jenny nestled against him, holding a handful of her hair across her face and breathing through it. The pickup's heater wasn't working properly, and her nose was cold. "Sam," she said, lifting her chin sharply. He looked where she was looking. By light flashing in circles from the snowplow's cab, Sam saw the fox crossing the lane, running just in front of the ice jetting from the slanted blade, and though the snowplow was coming slowly, the fox almost didn't make it—his head was cocked so that the black hen could rest, a dead weight, on his narrow shoulder, and he could not see where he was going, and he could not let go.

Listen to Reason

"Have you got a nickel?
Have you got a dime?
If your name is Nicholas,
You're—all—mine."

Driving, Charlie was still singing, nonsensically and softly, though by now he must have been singing for himself, because five-year-old Nicholas's face was moody in sleep and his jacket had fallen away from his shoulder. A gesture that Charlie resisted making repeated itself in his mind: his hand reaching to tug the jacket back up. An American, Charlie had a cautious sense of the dark English road before him. In London he took the underground; he'd never had to adapt to driving on the left, and there have been ruby-red eyes shining in the verge, reflecting the halogen brilliance of the Renault's headlights. Headlamps, if you wanted to think Englishly, but Charlie didn't. In the lowest dips of the road, mist had settled so densely the headlights could hardly pierce it.

His nothing songs for Nicholas meant exactly that—nothing—yet when Charlie brooded over this one, he found in it an accidental echo of his own father's declaration, when Charlie was small, that Charlie was going to nickel and dime him to death. This was said with that familiar confiding tilt of his father's head that had left Charlie believing he'd just been taken deeply, probably permanently, into his father's confidence, but Charlie had always believed wrong; he'd leaped too soon, when his father was only teasing, until finally Charlie had tired of leaping. When Charlie was nine and his father forty, cancer had come and swept away all of their normal, mutual chances for reconciliation. His father's death existed, a little live cinder of unhealing hurt, far back in Charlie's heart. This was what Charlie did not want his own son to live with, if (when) Charlie died: anger at having been left so incompletely understood.

If, when, he died. His mood had been bleak lately, though bleak moods were infrequent for Charlie.

He'd sworn he wouldn't leave England without visiting Hadrian's Wall, and Kyra had taken advantage of that, and of the fact that throughout their London year Charlie had spent cruelly little time with Nicholas, to pack father and son off in this rented Renault. Though he and Nicholas had been to Stonehenge only two weeks before, "cruelly little time" was Kyra's phrase, coined in a tearful, accusing rage. This trip also left her with what she said she needed, a long weekend alone to pack the last of their stuff for the Heathrow scramble. Their New York odds and ends had never fit in well with the dour English antiques that inhabited their chilly leased flat, and Charlie thought with relief of locking that narrow London door behind them for the last time. That they'd come to England at all was his fault. He'd been offered a year with a London publisher by his New York house, an offer too good to believe, then too good to refuse: Charlie's version, presented to his silent wife. Silent, but, he sensed, only half listening, so that Charlie's spirits rose. Kyra listened carefully indeed when she was going to fight.

Later, he wished she'd fought. Pennies were "pee" to
Nicholas now, and somehow, possibly from his sitter's son, he'd
adopted that high pitch of nervous inquiry with which English
schoolboys ended sentences. Worse, the righteous Scottish sitter
had reported that on occasion Nicholas stole. Small things: a
comb, a handkerchief with Victorian embroidery. Those, the
sitter conveyed with lilting disapproval, she hadn't minded
losing. She hadn't wanted to trouble Kyra with the news. Then
Nicholas stole a farthing because he liked its wren. That, the
sitter minded very much. The farthing had been saved for her
own boy. Its loss was traced to Nicholas, and furiously shamed,
he had gone to pry it from its hiding place under a seat cushion:
a ruckus that Charlie, returning late from the Bedford Square
suite of publisher's offices, had found himself blamed for by his
suddenly inconsolable wife. Stealing equaled stealing affection,
Nicholas believed he must steal affection because his *father* was
so unavailable, and Hadrian's Wall was Charlie's last chance
to right the year-long wrong he'd inflicted—Kyra's reasoning,
if you could call it reasoning.

Most of that year was behind them now. There was hardly
anything left to get through: they would make it home to New
York. Charlie breathed deep, watching the road, and tried to let
virtue loosen what seemed to be a knot, a handspan-wide, con-
stricting knot, of anguish in his chest.

> *"Oh Charlie he's my darling,*
> *Charlie he's a saint,*
> *But if your name is Nicholas,*
> *You like blue paint."*

A nothing song of Charlie's, singing itself in Kyra's head as
Brian's MG bowled down the hedgerowed lane. "Charlie he's
a saint" was funny, wasn't it? There was no warning hidden in
it. There couldn't be, because Charlie didn't know, Charlie

never would know, that there was anything wrong. Her conviction that he did know, that was her guilt talking, not reason. Needing comfort, she would have laid her head on Brian's shoulder, but the seat belt he insisted she wear restrained her. It was funny realizing so late, just before parting from him, that her English lover loved driving, especially driving fast, and that he resisted distraction while he was doing it.

Until lately, she'd been sure of her ability to distract him from anything. Brian was a slight, clearheaded person, orderly by nature—in spite of her, orderly. She'd known from the beginning that she was going to wage war on that quality in him, on his reasonableness and resourcefulness as well, though those were the very things that had drawn her to him. In the gloomy Indian restaurant where she'd first consented to sleep with him —consented to herself; he hadn't even as yet asked—she'd shaken her head extravagantly at a remark of his about Maggie Thatcher's strident voice, and felt her favorite earring unclasp and break on the parquet floor. She'd cupped the pieces in her palm, hating herself for the gesture she couldn't have helped— the line of argument she'd meant to follow was that "strident" was a sexist term directed at unruly women, women who exposed themselves. The silver design and the wafer of its silver backing would join that stash of fragments she'd have mended on that faraway day when she got home to New York. Among the responses she was aware of, staring down at the pieces, was this self-reproach: in London she never got around to getting anything fixed. London had nullified her, countered initiative, washed away her New York self and left her with nothing else. She looked up as, without asking, he tipped the two fragments from her hand into his. Nesting the design neatly in its backing, he bit the earring lightly two or three times to seal the fit. Fastening it back on her earlobe, she'd felt his saliva there.

· · ·

⟨ They were well into a small village when, from the corner of her eye, Kyra saw it: in the spring darkness it was another narrow English house, fronting the rain-pooled lane composedly, giving nothing away. When Brian drove by it, she thought in disappointment, Oh, wrong one. It was only when the village petered out into dark fields again and he halted the MG, shaking his head, saying, "You'll think I'm an idiot," that she knew she'd been right, that had been the house where they were expected. She laughed, and teased the corner of his mouth with a gloved finger until he forgot himself enough to smile. He still hated making mistakes in front of her, and she still craved them from him, as proof that he was no longer so self-reliantly clear-headed after all.

In the car, idling in the cold field with its sullen feedlot smell of rained-on manure, he put his palms against her cheekbones so so that his fingers were in her hair, and rocked her head back and forth so that she seemed to be saying *no no no.* This was a habit of his lately. Was it a parody of her way of denying him things, limiting their relationship, keeping its end always before his eyes? The top was down, the damp wind was blowing her hair into her face, and he cleared the strands away, saying, "You can shake your head all you like, but I'm coming to New York next summer. I've decided."

This had come up before. Her usual response was to draw a red herring across that path, to sidetrack him in such a way that the sidetracking felt final, but recently she'd been finding this harder to do. As her flight to New York and safety drew nearer, it was her emotions that were unruly, that had begun catching her off guard. This trip, when she'd never granted him so much time before, made her feel more than usually precarious: what had she gotten herself into, and why?

Before she could think of an answer for him, he had the MG in reverse and moving fast enough so that the flat black fields whipped away and were replaced by dense hedgerows. He backed over a bridge resonant with the buckling sound of sodden old wood, then accelerated hard, startling her, where the lane gleamed under the first somber housefronts. These ancient houses were steep and dark with disapproval, a strict, unforgiving village parting crookedly down the middle to let the MG careen through insanely backwards. She stared over her shoulder, tears rinsing horizontally across her cheeks, and because her fist had lodged itself against her teeth, she sucked her knuckles, willing him to make no mistakes, willing her reflexes magically to second his. For fear of distracting him she made no sound. In the taillights' blaze, close under the rear tires, a mouse dashed across the black-glass asphalt, *safe*. When the car lurched she didn't feel it as a skid. It was more as if the MG's body jarred sideways and there was one floating, eternal instant before the tires caught and were snug underneath it again, the tailpipe grinding down along a rise in the road with a long, rusty rasp magnified by the wet silence in which the rest of this occurred. The MG hugged backwards around another tight curve, past a small church, then threaded the needle of lane between high walls, the taillights dazzling the close-set flints into an array of quick, moving lights. The glaze of wet road steadied, the houses slowed, their sills and lamps and shutters stood out distinct. It was quiet, though she could have sworn a moment ago that someone had shouted out at them in a rage. Brian eased the car into the curb, really only an inadvertent shelving the road made below the flint housefront Kyra had noticed before because its window was lit.

One gentle, gauze-white window, shining into the street so peaceably it might have been the center of the world. Kyra waited for Brian to move. When he did, it was to lean toward her and put his arms around her. When she didn't react, he gently dug his shoulder under her chin so that her chin was raised and he could breathe appalled apology—"I'm sorry, so sorry"—down into her hair. The shout she had heard before started up again, in her head. A voice was shouting to her that he could have *killed* Charlie's wife, Nicholas's mother.

《 Inside the flint house, there was the echo-y, premonitory silence of adults keeping quiet for the sake of baby sleep. With painful alertness to the impression they were making, Kyra and Brian seated themselves on the leather sofa, only they sat down too near each other and had to rise, awkwardly together, and reseat themselves. If big, curly-headed Simon, judiciously feeding the flames in the tiled fireplace, observed the strain in this lovers' comedy routine, he gave no sign. He was Brian's oldest friend, and had seen him through the long-drawn-out dissolution of his relationship with an actress, Pippa. Though when Brian told her this, Kyra wondered how much seeing through Brian, being Brian, had ever needed.

"It smells beautiful," Kyra said, of the smoke wafting from the too small fireplace; the entire house was on such a tiny scale that she felt as if the dramatic, soot-darkened beams in the white plaster ceiling were close above her head.

Simon, kneeling, turned toward her. "Do you know what we burn now?" His tone was accusing. He answered himself: "Our elms. All our ruined, our dead and dying elms," and Kyra felt, spreading out behind her, a luxuriant forest of unscathed American trees. Upstairs, a baby began to squall, furiously loud.

Simon said sourly, "It's not the air-raid siren at all, it's Joseph."

In a detached way, as if to deflect Simon's mysterious anger from herself, Kyra traced a seam in the leather and, down between the cushions, found a pacifier still bearing the crimp of Joseph's gums. "Ah," Simon said, "thank you, I'll take that," and extracted it from her fingers. Only then did she realize she'd been looking at it wistfully, and was embarrassed.

"Sounds in an excellent mood," Brian said, of the wailing from above; he was as self-contained as ever, and Kyra had no idea how he felt. In the car, in the cold street, she'd refused to forgive him. She'd almost refused to come into this house at all, until he convinced her that there was really no alternative, that it would be absurd for them to drive back to London tonight.

"He's just tuning up," Simon said. "More to come, I'm afraid, unless Fiona manages a miracle. She sometimes does."

Kyra wished bitterly that someone would sometime observe of her, so matter-of-factly, "She sometimes does," and understood with a start that she was jealous of this household, and of Fiona, as yet unseen.

Simon handed Kyra a drink and found his hostility of a moment ago ridiculous. What was it in Brian's women that sometimes brought it out in him, this rush of aggrieved aggression? Kyra rested the glass along her lower lip, then drank. She had dark hair, and the way it fell along her fine forehead and under her jaw proved there was no harm in her, none. Either she had a cold or she'd been crying, for her eyes were raw. Crying, Simon decided. Protectiveness gusted through him. What messes Brian got people into.

Simon was still observing Kyra when her mouth shaped a soft, shy O and Fiona entered, the baby braced against her shoulder. Simon and Brian exchanged a long look that neither could have interpreted easily, and Fiona did something backed by that stunning simplicity only she was capable of: bending forward, with a dislodging, easing twist of her shoulder, she handed the baby to Kyra, who rose to receive it. At almost the same instant, the women breathed to each other over the baby's head, "Hello," and "Hallo," and then Fiona said, "He's bored to tears with me." Joseph was in Kyra's arms, and she said mindlessly, "Oh, hey, you're heavier than you look."

"Baby-worship time," Simon said, not sourly, but on a note of graceful irony.

Joseph's breath, panting from tiny apple-seed nostrils against Kyra's face when she held him propped upright by his bottom, had a sweetness that stirred her stomach queasily; well, she'd felt nauseated in the car from Brian's stupidity. For an instant she hated the old cloth draped over her shoulder by Fiona, with sleight-of-hand deftness, in case he burped up; she disliked the way his baggy baby cheek was squashed in by her cheekbone when he bumbled his face to rest against hers. He caught a handful of her hair and yanked, which made her want to snarl into his pink cowrie ear. Turning heftily she looked anxiously at Brian, who drew her down onto the sofa and began to extricate her hair from Joseph's sticky fist. Fiona had disappeared into the kitchen.

"He's not willing to let you go, darling," Brian said. "Darling" roused her fury at him afresh. Kyra stood, and because the two men were sitting, standing conferred on her sudden princess status, and Joseph of an instant grew manageable, a blond baby boy-toy to flirt in her arms in front of the two men. It was as if they were both in love with her. Kyra put her dark forehead against Joseph's very fair one, guessing the picture this would make, and Joseph, more deceived than anyone by this act, opened his eyes absolutely round, and she sensed, within her uneasiness at being here at all, the faint pleasurable dawning of possessiveness, light at first and then mounting almost to a pressure, so that she forgot he was being studied and simply held Joseph, moving her lips in the down of his head, seeing the fair strands wave with her breath. Kyra began that standing-rocking, rolling into her left hip, cocking it, then rolling into the right, a self- and baby-seductive motion she could have carried on for an hour, and right in her arms Joseph gave up his war and fell asleep.

⟨ Wine in glasses that had been Fiona's great-grandmother's, and salad, and glossy black mussels in a bowl. "Careful," said Simon, "there's a duff one on top," because you weren't supposed to eat those whose shells were slightly agape. To finish, cheese, crackers, and port. When Kyra turned down the Brie, three English voices insisted: She must at least try it. At last Simon cleared the table while Fiona finished her wine and, with apologies for their being a weary old married couple, they went upstairs, leaving their guests the empty table, the wine bottle, and the small fire flickering across the quarry-tile floor. Brian stroked Kyra's hair and said, mock-accusingly, "You liked them." In London, when he'd told her how he wanted to spend this last, lied-for weekend, she'd been sure she would be nervous around this couple. "More inexplicable still," he said, "they liked you."

"You can tell, with Simon?"

Brian laughed. "He is a riddle, when first you meet him."

"He was so angry about the elms. I got a kind of 'our tiny island, your huge imperialist continent' feeling from that."

"I shouldn't hold it against him. I doubt he meant that."

"I can't be manipulated out of knowing what I felt," she said, and she waited for him to ask, "Felt about?"

Instead he traced her lower lip with a knuckle, studying her to see how much she disliked him at this particular moment, and something in her small, set face decided him, because he put his palms to her cheekbones, asking, "Make love?" and shook her head for her, *no no no.*

"Back to London would have been a good idea," she said.

"It wasn't possible," he said.

❨ Kyra woke startled in Brian's arms, her cheek to his pale
English chest, to find that Fiona was bringing them tea.
Right into the tiny guest bedroom.

Fiona put the tray down, kneeling among their fallen
clothes, and aligned the teacup handles before pouring the tea.
Her hair, the shade of her son's, swung over her face. Kyra
closed her eyes and pretended to be asleep because that was
slightly less embarrassing than being awake for this, and Brian
said softly, "Thank you; it looks marvelous," to Fiona, who left,
shutting the door nicely behind her. Brian's bathrobe fell from
the door as it closed, and he jumped from the bed, padding across
their tumbled things, and put it on before handing Kyra
her tea.

She sat up in bed, balancing the cup and saucer on her
knees. "I don't forgive you for the car, you know." She meant:
Even though we made love, it wasn't me forgiving you.

"I think you do," he said. He meant, she thought: You
couldn't have held real resentment through our making love like
that. She shook her head, spilling tea into her saucer, and he
said, "Mind Fiona's sheets."

"That was dangerous of you."

"Kyra, I've driven that lane for years, in all kinds of weather.
I know it thoroughly."

"You can't." Her logic felt like a death ray she was about
to aim at him, and since it had usually gone the other way—he
annihilating some argument of hers with his formidable reasonableness—she felt pity for him, and an understanding coldness.
"You drove right by the house."

"That was preoccupation, not a lack of—of familiarity with
the place." He finished most of his tea, and all of his biscuits.
She gave him hers. She hated biscuits first thing in the morning.
In spite of her, they were almost on the brink of reconciliation.

She fished for the last of the anger she still truly felt, and said, "I don't want to stay."

"We were supposed to have the weekend. There's lots I wanted you to see. You're not only disappointing me," he said, "you'll be disappointing them."

His playing on a guilt he thought she could be made to feel made things easier. She was glad he'd done it. Whether she was angry at him or not, she should be; she wanted to be, and she wanted to go home.

⟨ The little car was purring away in an effort to keep up the level of its tepid interior heat, and its windshield wipers, in quick, clocking strokes, showed the rainy, empty street before Kyra's flat. Brian had already shuttled her things from the trunk of the car into the sheltered entryway before her building's locked doors, and sitting in the car with him was making her nervous, but she held her tongue out of some idea that she owed him a last-minute explanation.

The problem was, he wasn't allowing her to make anything sound final. His patience with her extended itself deftly, counteringly, before any move she thought to make. Often before, this tactic had kept her from making a definitive break with him, but she did not really see how either one of them could fail to accept that now, today, was definitive.

"New York is out," she said. She meant his visit to New York.

"All right," he said. "Why?"

"Because I want my life to be all in one piece," she said. "Not part in New York, part here. Can you understand that?"

"I understand that Nicholas is the biggest piece."

She let him have it that way: Nicholas was a reason he could accept.

"It's just sudden," he said. "I thought we'd have the whole

weekend. To talk. To wander round. I thought we'd come to some other conclusion."

"I know you wanted that to happen, but it wouldn't have."

"You believe that," he said. "I think it would have done. And isn't it you who accuses *me* of deliberately ignoring what she feels to be true?"

She looked out at her street. "All right," she said. "You think two more days would have changed things."

"Yes."

《 Midway through the flight, on an airplane crowded with 《 sleepers, she rested her chin against Nicholas's head and whispered, "From now on you have to be good." She caught in Charlie's reading profile the absentminded, mild smile with which, even though he wasn't truly listening, he monitored the tone of her voice; she counted this smile as a gift, a stroke of luck, because it was a smile of contented, if uncomprehending, possessiveness. Toward her, she knew, and Nicholas. She chose her moment. He turned a page. She said, "Charlie, I want a second child."

Without quite taking his eyes from the page, he said, "I always wondered how that decision got reached." With his gaze downcast, his upper lip somehow longer than usual, the way it was when he was reading as an editor, he added, "I mean, to have a second child."

She said, "Maybe it's like all other decisions: you only know it's a decision when you find yourself acting on it."

He answered, "Maybe," with a touch of consternation she must unwittingly have caused, turning toward her. He went on, "What made you decide now?"

She said softly, "You," and touching Nicholas's dreaming head, "and him," and remembering what other reasons there had been, she had cause to be glad that Charlie, locked into his private shaft of reading light, could not see her clearly for the shadow; seen even briefly, even slantwise, her face would have given her away.

Yet it would come to haunt her how often, in the weeks and months that followed, she dreamed she was back inside the speeding car.

A NOTE ON THE TYPE

The text of this book was set on the Linotype in a type face known as Garamond. The design is based on letter forms originally created by Claude Garamond (c.1480–1561). Garamond was a pupil of Geoffroy Tory and may have patterned his letter forms on Venetian models. To this day, the type face that bears his name is one of the most attractive used in book composition, and the intervening years have caused it to lose little of its freshness or beauty.

Composed by Maryland Linotype Composition Company, Baltimore, Maryland

Printed and bound by The Haddon Craftsmen, Inc., Scranton, Pennsylvania

*Typography and binding design by
Claire M. Naylon*